"You've Changed, Arlette.

"In those tailored slacks and that silk blouse, you look every inch the city slicker."

Trust Julian not to say anything about how long she had been away or wasn't it nice she was back or any of those civilized pleasantries. Instead, he had zeroed in unerringly on the source of her greatest insecurity: whether she would be able to find a place for herself in the bayous. With a handful of well-chosen words he had immediately put her on the defensive. Or he would have, if she had gone along with him, something she wasn't about to do.

"Talk about change, Julian, life must be treating you well. It looks as though you've put on a few pounds."

Reflexively, he looked down at his flat stomach. He shook his head. "No, I don't think I have." Looking up again, he saw her smile and realized she was teasing. A low laugh broke from him. "Forget what I said. You haven't changed at all."

Dear Reader,

Welcome to Silhouette! Our goal is to give you hours of unbeatable reading pleasure, and we hope you'll enjoy each month's six new Silhouette Desires. These sensual, provocative love stories are both believable and compelling—sometimes they're poignant, sometimes humorous, but always enjoyable.

Indulge yourself. Experience all the passion and excitement of falling in love along with our heroine as she meets the irresistible man of her dreams and together they overcome all obstacles in the path to a happy ending.

If this is your first Desire, I hope it'll be the first of many. If you're already a Silhouette Desire reader, thanks for your support! Look for some of your favorite authors in the coming months: Stephanie James, Diana Palmer, Dixie Browning, Ann Major and Doreen Owens Malek, to name just a few.

Happy reading!

Isabel Swift
Senior Editor

SDRL-7/85

MAURA SEGER
Cajun Summer

Silhouette Desire

Published by Silhouette Books New York

America's Publisher of Contemporary Romance

SILHOUETTE BOOKS
300 East 42nd St., New York, N.Y.   10017

Copyright © 1986 by Maura Seger

ISBN: 0-373-05282-0

First Silhouette Books printing May 1986

America's Publisher of Contemporary Romance

Printed in the U.S.A.

MAURA SEGER

was prompted by a love of books and a vivid imagination to decide, at age twelve, to be a writer. Twenty years later, her first book was published. So much, she says, for overnight success! Now she finds each book is an adventure, filled with fascinating people who always surprise her.

One

There was nothing so disconcerting as having one's expectations fulfilled, Arlette Dumas decided as she stood on the corner of Arkady, Louisiana's main street.

A soft breeze off the bayou ruffled her chestnut hair and added a touch of color to high-boned cheeks that were otherwise pale. Her blue eyes were pensive as she looked up and down the dusty road that was framed by ramshackle buildings and didn't stretch further than an average city block.

Directly across from her was the Bons Temps Bar, in front of which the three-times-weekly bus to Morgan City stopped. The bus had been and gone a few minutes before, pausing only long enough for the driver to unload a few packages. No passengers had gotten off or on.

Arlette wondered if the overall-clad men who always seemed to be seated on the bench out in front of the bar were disappointed. Probably not, since almost no one ever came or went in Arkady. She was the exception to that.

Next to the bar was the hardware store, and a little farther down the street was the Cajun Cafe. On the side where she stood were the service station, a grocery store that also served as the post office, and the shack where boats were repaired and tackle sold. Behind the buildings was a sagging wooden dock. Dark green water lapped at its crumbling pilings.

Not more than fifty yards in either direction the town faded back into the bayou, the vast, shadowy marsh that had existed for thousands of years before people ever came to call it home and would remain long after the last of them was gone.

Arlette shook her head slowly as she brushed a strand of hair from her damp forehead. Another thing that hadn't changed was the weather. Summer in the bayou had always been hot and sultry; this one was no exception.

Many times during the eight years she had been away she told herself not to be disappointed by the changes time must surely have wrought, yet she could never quite believe that everything wouldn't be exactly as she remembered. Now it seemed her faith had been justified. Arkady was just as it had always been; she might have been away only a day or an hour, instead of what seemed almost to be a lifetime.

That troubled her. She had been counting on external changes to remind her of how different she was from the troubled young girl who had fled her home not knowing if she would ever be able to return. Now she had, but not without full awareness of the risks. For the sake of everything she had won in the time away, nothing could really be the same.

"Penny for 'em," a deep voice said beside her. She turned, looking up into the gentle brown eyes of her brother. An embarrassed smile curved her mouth.

"Sorry, Louis, you caught me daydreaming."

"That's all right, Sis. I guess in your shoes I'd be a little distracted too. Oncle Pierre says he can fix the outboard, but I'll have to leave it a few days. Want to head on home?"

Arlette nodded. She was surprised that the brief excursion into town had made her feel so tired, but she put it down to the long hours of travel the day before. From New York she had flown to New Orleans, where she had rented a car and driven the last hundred or so miles to Arkady.

It was a trip she had planned to make dozens of times during her years away, but something had always stopped her. At first it was the grueling regimen of college, where she had to study almost constantly to maintain a high enough average to keep her scholarship, while also holding down a part-time job waiting tables.

Then there was graduate school, where conditions were much the same, except that she was also expected to teach. After that had come the two years working in New York, during which she had thought more and more of going home. Finally, after several exchanges of letters and phone calls, she had been confident enough of her welcome to take the risk.

Still, it had been very difficult to get on that plane. She had come very close to chickening out. Only the deepest desire for reconciliation with her family had prevented her from doing so.

Her brother seemed to instinctively understand that. At twenty-five, Louis was the younger by a year. His six-foot-plus height topped hers by at least a head, and his brawny build contrasted sharply with her slender shapeliness. Yet brother and sister were alike in the quiet firmness of their natures and the steadfastness with which they clung to their goals.

"Are you seeing Debbie tonight?" Arlette asked as they walked back toward the rickety pickup that had brought them into town. Her blue eyes beneath spiky lashes gleamed mischievously. Despite the years away, her relationship with her brother had resumed as though nothing had happened to interrupt it. Already they had begun teasing each other mercilessly, just as when they were children.

Louis blushed faintly beneath his habitual tan and jiggled the keys in the pocket of his jeans. "Maybe. Depends on whether or not I've got something better to do."

Arlette laughed, her heart-shaped face alive with amusement. "Like what? I don't imagine there are too many things that would keep you away from sweet little Deborah."

Her brother cast her a knowing glance as he grinned. "She's not so little, or so sweet. Truth be told, she can be a real spitfire when she wants to be."

"Good for her," Arlette said firmly. "I'm glad she stands up to you. Too many girls around here still cater to a man's every whim."

"Maybe they know something you don't," Louis shot back, his tone light.

"Fat chance," Arlette scoffed. "I know better than to spend my life trailing after some man, waiting for him to notice I'm around and throw me a few crumbs. That's no way to live." Despite herself, she couldn't quite keep a note of bitterness from her voice.

Louis heard it and stopped. He touched her arm lightly. "It's okay, Sis. No one expects this to be easy for you."

She bit her lip, looking over his broad shoulder at nothing in particular. "I'm sorry. I didn't mean to come on so strong."

"You don't," he assured her. "Besides, what you say makes sense. I couldn't stand a woman trying to live in my pocket instead of making her own life."

Arlette laughed faintly. "You keep talking like that and I'll think women's liberation has come to the bayou."

"Not quite," Louis admitted, "but attitudes have changed some since we were growing up. It used to be people thought there was only one right way to be. They see alternatives now they didn't used to consider."

Arlette wondered about that even as she tried hard not to. The memory of how it had been to find herself caught in the remorseless grip of expectations she could not fulfill still had the power to hurt her.

Eight years before, she had been faced with the choice of being true to herself or of following a way of life she loved but couldn't fully accept. She had chosen to follow her own dreams, and had never really regretted that decision, but the consequences had been harsh.

"I need to stop at the post office before we go home," she said.

"Okay. Why don't you go on ahead while I drop by the hardware store? Dad asked me to pick up a few things."

Arlette agreed, and they parted on the sidewalk. Entering the grocery store, she paused to glance at the racks of spices, kitchenware, and brightly colored fabric piled high on wooden shelves. The smell of sawdust and the soft lapping of the nearby bayou conjured up memories from her childhood. She had only to close her eyes to see herself as a little girl, sitting cross-legged on the floor playing jacks while her mother got her shopping list filled and chatted with the other women.

They had been good days, filled with sunlight, the safety of routine, and above all the certainty of being loved. But they hadn't made growing up any easier, at least not for her.

"There you are," the old woman behind the counter at the back of the store said, her voice high and thin with age, yet still vigorous. "I heard you were back. Come on over here, honey, and let me get a closer look at you."

With a slight smile, Arlette obliged. Evangeline Cartier was a grandmother and great-grandmother so many times over it was possible even she did not know the full count of her progeny. By virtue of her venerable age and her long friendship with Arlette's family, she was entitled to her curiosity.

"You're thinner, child," Evangeline said as she surveyed the young woman. "Didn't they feed you up north?"

"Not the way Mom does," Arlette assured her with a smile. "I expect I'll fill out now that I'm back."

"Planning on staying?" Evangeline asked as she rummaged behind the counter.

"For a while...it depends on how soon I get a job."

"Might be something here for you about that." Handing over a small stack of letters, the old woman added, "They're all from big companies in places like Morgan City and New Orleans. There's even one from Houston." Her pale gray eyes were alight with speculation.

"Thanks," Arlette murmured dryly. She couldn't find it in her to be upset by Evangeline's snooping, knowing as she did that it was well meant. A certain lack of privacy was one of the things she would have to get used to for however long she remained in Arkady. In such a small tightly knit community, people inevitably tended to be very interested in each other.

She glanced through the letters quickly, then chatted a few minutes longer before taking her leave. Back on the sidewalk, she looked around for Louis, saw that he wasn't in sight, and opened the topmost envelope.

Inside was a letter from an oil and gas company in New Orleans, sent in response to her inquiry of a few weeks before. As she quickly scanned the neatly typed paragraphs she was relieved to note that her résumé had been considered "impressive" and the personnel director looked forward to discussing several "opportunities" with her. He closed by suggesting that she call for an appointment.

A small surge of excitement darted through her. She felt that she was off to a good start and didn't hesitate to open the rest of the envelopes. Not all the letters were as encouraging—several regretfully cited a lack of open staff positions—but three more asked her to get in touch to set up interviews.

The hopes she had for finding a job that would make good use of her skills as a geologist now seemed more than justified. It was with a buoyant sense of self-confidence that she started down the street toward the truck, only to stop abruptly when she caught sight of the man striding toward her from the opposite direction.

The sun was behind him, casting his tall, powerfully built figure into silhouette, but she was still absolutely certain of his identity. No one else walked with quite that degree of deceptively leisurely grace, as though he were in no particular hurry to get wherever he might be going because everything there would wait for him.

For a brief instant she considered darting back inside the grocery store and hoping that he would pass by without noticing her. But that was the coward's way out, and Arlette had never been one to run from a challenge. Thinking that perhaps she would have been better off if she had been, she stepped forward and smiled.

"Hello, Julian. It's nice to see you again."

The tall, ebony-haired man stopped and looked at her. His hazel eyes, deeply set beneath curving brows, surveyed her slender form and finely molded features with a hint of puzzlement, as though he was trying unsuccessfully to place her.

That went on just long enough for her to ache at the thought that he might not remember her. Then his puzzlement vanished, and he returned her smile, cautiously.

"You've changed, Arlette. In those tailored slacks and that silk blouse, you look every inch the city slicker."

Trust Julian not to say anything about how long she had been away, or wasn't it nice that she was back, or any of those civilized pleasantries. Instead he had zeroed in unerringly on the source of her greatest insecurity: whether or not she would be able to find a place for herself again in the bayous. With a handful of well-chosen words he had immediately put her on the defensive.

Or at least he would have if she went along with him, something she was not about to do.

"Talk about change, Julian. Life must be treating you well. It looks as though you've put on a few pounds."

The fathomless eyes that had once so fascinated her narrowed in surprise. Reflexively, he looked down at his flat stomach beneath the denim workshirt he wore tucked into chinos. He shook his head, and sunlight silvered the ebony strands of his hair. "No, I don't think I have." Looking up again he saw the tremor of a smile at the corners of her mouth and realized she was teasing.

A low laugh broke from him. "Forget what I said. You haven't changed at all. I should know better than to try to get the better of you."

But he alway had, and the memory of that took her smile away, replacing it with a softness that held a hint of regret. "How long has it been...?" she asked, knowing full well when they had last seen each other. The memory of that final encounter was etched on her memory as though with acid.

"Eight years." He slid his hands into the back pockets of his slacks and continued to study her. His square jaw was set in an unrelenting line she remembered only too well. "I hear you're a geologist."

She shrugged, distantly aware that faces had appeared at various windows. They were being eyed with interest. "I have a piece of paper with that on it, plus a couple of years' experience. I hope to line up the right job soon."

"You shouldn't have any trouble. Good geologists are always in demand."

She hoped he was correct, but didn't say so. There had been a time when she had confided everything in him, only to come to regret it.

"So you're going to be around for a while," he said, as though settling that in his own mind.

"A few weeks, perhaps. Not all the time, of course. I'll be back and forth on interviews."

"Of course." He smiled faintly, mocking her. "Your family must be glad."

"They seem happy to see me," she said carefully, hoping he didn't intend to say anything about how much she had been missed, or ask whether or not leaving had been worth all the heartache it had caused.

Julian considered saying both, but thought better of it. Once he wouldn't have hesitated to blurt out whatever came to his mind. He supposed that was how Arlette remembered him.

Eight years before he'd been twenty-three, and headstrong in a way only poverty coupled to ambition could create. He had known he would rise far above the place ordained by his birth simply because the alternative was unthinkable. What he hadn't known was that the price would be so high.

"What about your folks?" Arlette asked suddenly. "How are they?"

Julian hesitated. The coolly beautiful woman standing before him was so hauntingly familiar that she made his body throb with remembered need, yet she was also very different, almost a stranger. Every instinct he possessed told him to be wary of her, both for pain that had been and worse pain that might be.

"My mother died six years ago," he said quietly, "and Pa took off a while after that. I've got no idea where he went, can't say I care."

Her eyes, which he had always privately likened to the color of a summer sky after a freshening rain, darkened. Softly she said, "I'm sorry."

He dismissed her sympathy with a quick shrug of his broad shoulders. "Let's face it, we were never a close family." Almost unwillingly, he added, "Not like yours."

"No... not like mine." She really didn't need to be reminded of how much her family had meant to Julian. Sometimes she had wondered which he cared for more, them or her. Only toward the end had she realized that in Julian's mind there was no difference. He had wanted it all. And he had gotten... what?

"What brings you back here?" she asked. "Just visiting?"

"Not exactly.... I had business in the area so I decided to stay awhile."

"Are you out at your folks' place?" She didn't want to think of him staying in the dirty, dilapidated shack that had once been his only home. But perhaps he had fixed it up.

He shook his head. "Near there." Before she could ask anything further, he caught sight of Louis coming out of the hardware store and raised a hand.

"How you doing, kid?"

Her brother surveyed them both for a moment before he grinned. "Not too bad. How about yourself?"

"Fine, just fine. I see Arlette's back."

"For a while. She's looking for a job."

The object of their comments frowned. They were talking about her as though she wasn't even there, which really shouldn't surprise her, since it had gone on often enough before. Only now she had no patience with it. "If you don't mind," she broke in, "I think we ought to be getting home. Mom will be expecting us for supper."

"Yeah, you're right," Louis said, reluctantly. She guessed he wanted to talk further with Julian and regretted pulling him away, but was determined nonetheless.

Except that her brother apparently had other thoughts. "Hey," he said to Julian, "how about joining us? Mom and Dad would love to see you, and it's never any trouble to set another plate."

"I couldn't—" Julian began.

"He undoubtedly has other plans," Arlette broke in.

Their eyes met, his darkly thoughtful, hers glittering with silent challenge. That was a mistake. Like her, he had never been one to take the easy way out. "Well, no," he said after a moment, "actually I don't."

"It's settled then," Louis decided. "You can ride over with us."

Julian promptly agreed, leaving Arlette with no choice but to follow him and her brother as they strolled toward the pickup. Her silent fuming went unnoticed as they all climbed in, Arlette squeezed in the middle. The motor coughed to life reluctantly.

"Is this the same truck I remember?" Julian asked. He had one arm propped on the rolled down window; the other lay on top of the seat behind Arlette. Try though she did, she could not ignore his nearness.

The warmth of his body reached out to her, along with the subtle, unique scent of him and the unmistakable aura of strength he had always projected, even in her dreams. Against the nape of her neck, she could feel the corded muscles of his forearm, reminding her all too easily of when she had known the fullness of his strength. She flushed and stared straight ahead, determined that he should not know what was going through her mind.

Louis laughed softly. "The one and only. Pa was going to get rid of her, but I talked him into letting me overhaul her instead. Runs fine now." As he spoke, gears ground shrilly and a plume of exhaust spewed out of the tail pipe.

"Fine?" Arlette repeated dubiously. "In New York they won't even run buses in this condition and, believe me, that's really saying something."

"That so?" Louis drawled with a quick look at Julian. Over her head, the two men grinned at each other. "Well, now, I can't claim to know anything 'bout what goes on in the big city. You'll have to tell us all 'bout it."

Arlette rolled her eyes heavenward. "Give me strength. Ever since I got home you've been playing the country bumpkin. How about easing up a little?"

"Sorry, Sis," her brother said good-naturedly. "You know I never could resist teasing you. Remember that time I told her there was a monster out by the woodshed that liked to eat little girls?" he asked Julian.

"Do I ever. It took me a good two weeks to convince her that wasn't true."

"I was seven years old at the time," Arlette protested. "Of course I got scared."

"And went scampering to Julian," her brother added. "Just like you always did." He glanced over at the other man, who seemed to be thoroughly enjoying the ride. "Didn't you ever get tired of her doing that?"

"Not really," Julian said, ignoring Arlette's irate snort. "Oh, she got in the way from time to time, but I didn't really mind. Truth is I kind of liked having her around."

"At least I was an improvement over those girls you used to date," Arlette broke in. "For one thing, I could walk and chew gum at the same time."

"I went out with some very nice young ladies," Julian said chidingly, "before you grew up and started taking all my time."

"Ladies? If they were ladies, I'm a—"

"We're almost there," Louis broke in. "Mom will about split when she sees who I brought home. Why, hardly a week goes by that she doesn't mention your name, Julian."

Arlette sighed and subsided back against the seat. Her brother's none-too-subtle efforts to remind them of what they had once shared were understandable, given how fond her family had always been of Julian, but that didn't mean she knew how to cope with the situation.

She squirmed slightly, wondering if Louis's attitude would be any different if he knew exactly how close she and Julian had been. Much as her brother claimed to approve of more modern values and morals, she knew that at heart he remained as protective toward the women of his family as every true Cajun male. Yet, she reminded herself, he was no monk himself and might well have guessed more than she wanted to admit.

From beneath her lashes she dared a quick glance at Julian. His head was thrown back as he laughed at something Louis had just said. Watching the powerful muscles ripple in the corded column of his throat, she felt a wave of heat wash over her that had nothing to do with the languid summer day.

Memories flowed unbidden through her mind, sweet yet sharp in their poignant intensity, the fleeting glimpses of a cherished dream that had been briefly fulfilled, only to be cruelly shattered.

Two

It seemed as though Julian had alway been a part of her life, perhaps the central part, despite her closeness to her family. He was there in her earliest recollections, at first as a remote figure seen only on the periphery of her awareness, but swiftly coming to dominate all her horizons.

As a child she had instinctively sought to draw him inside the warm, bright circle of love her family provided and his so clearly did not. Yet she had never pitied him.

Even as a boy, he had been exceptionally strong and determined. More times than she could remember she had sought comfort from him, and he had always given it. Finally, he had also learned to let her reciprocate.

By the time Arlette was twelve, Julian was a man of eighteen, mature in a way her brother was not. He had seemed closer in certain respects to her father, even though Charlie Dumas was more than two decades his senior. The two of them had often sat on the porch for hours talking after everyone else had gone to bed.

Arlette had sometimes snuck halfway down the stairs and sat with her nightgown tucked around her, listening to the soft rise and fall of male voices. She had envied her father for having Julian's confidence, wanting it as she did for herself.

When she was sixteen the nature of her relationship with Julian had abruptly changed. Ten years later she still blushed to remember the circumstances.

She'd been out on a date with a boy who had seemed nice enough but turned out to be anything but. When she refused to give him what he wanted, he'd tried to force her, then finally given up and left her stranded on a lonely country road miles from home. The pretty blue dress she'd put on with such pride had been torn in several places, she'd lost the heel to one of her shoes, and bruises were already darkening on her shoulders and arms as she limped along.

Looking back, she supposed she must have been quite a sight, which was apparently what Julian thought when he happened across her on his way from work. As usual, he'd done two shifts back to back in the oil fields and was bone tired. Yet when he screeched his car to a halt beside her and jumped out, all she could think of was how blessedly strong and safe he looked.

Until, that is, he spoke. Never in her life had she heard such implacable coldness as he demanded, "Who did this to you?"

Brushing a tear away with the back of her hand, she had told him, all the while wondering why he didn't take her into his arms and give her the comfort she so badly needed. Instead he had merely stared at her relentlessly, taking in every detail of her battered appearance, before he finally said, "Come on."

"Wh-where are we going?" she asked shakily as she followed him.

He opened the car door on the passenger side, thrust her in, and slammed it hard, then walked around the front of the car to get behind the wheel. Not until he had gunned the motor did he answer. "Home, of course. Your parents don't deserve this, but they have to know."

"Don't deserve . . . but it wasn't my fault!"

"You went out with the guy, didn't you?"

"He seemed very nice," she protested, her fear and exhaustion fading before a healthy spurt of anger. "How was I supposed to know he was going to come on like an octopus? Next you'll be telling me I asked for it." Her voice broke as she looked away, hating for him to see her cry.

Julian muttered a curse that under other circumstances would have shocked her, but which she hardly noticed. He yanked hard on the wheel, pulling the car onto the side of the road, then leaned over and scooped her into his arms. She was in his lap, her body cradled against his, before she knew what had happened.

"I'm sorry," he said thickly, "I had no right treating you like that. You're not to blame."

She lifted her head from his shoulder despite his efforts to keep it there. Her eyes were luminous with tears that trickled down her pale cheeks. "I know I'm not. But I feel so..." She broke off, not sure what she was feeling, much less how to explain it to him.

"I understand," he said softly, stroking her hair. "You're afraid you can't trust your own judgment anymore, but everyone's entitled to make mistakes. You have to chalk it up to experience and be glad you got off as lightly as you did."

He hesitated a moment before his long, blunt-tipped fingers eased beneath her chin and he tilted her head back gently. His chiseled features were taut with apprehension as he asked, "You did, didn't you?"

She flushed when she realized what he meant. "When he found out I wouldn't . . . you know . . . he pushed me out of the car. That's all."

Julian nodded grimly. "That was enough. You've got to be more careful from now on, honey. Some guys just can't be trusted around a beautiful girl."

The pain of her bruises and the fear still lurking within were forgotten as she focused on what he had just said. "Do you really think I'm beautiful?"

"You know you are."

"No . . . I don't know." She laughed self-consciously. "I'm only sixteen, too young to know much of anything."

He grinned. "You said it, not me."

Anger was gone, and fear with it. There was only a sweet sense of rightness as she tilted her head slightly, waiting, hoping, tentative as a bird about to light on a branch and not sure its perch would be steady.

Julian hesitated a moment, then seemed to reach some crucial decision within himself. He took her mouth with a thoroughness that stunned even as it unleashed a torrent of feeling unlike anything she had ever before experienced.

She had been kissed a few times by boys, which was to say she had not been kissed at all. Never had she known the heady urgency of true passion made all the more intense by the absolute control he exhibited. A soft moan rippled from her as she arched closer to him, parting her lips to let him more fully savor the inner warmth of her mouth.

Julian's arms tightened around her, not hurtfully, but with pressure that reminded her of his great strength. In his embrace she felt infinitely safe and protected, yet also free to experience the heady delights of her womanhood. Until he abruptly drew back, his face flushed and a ragged pulse beating in the hollow of his shadowed cheek.

"I have no sense around you, Arlette," he murmured huskily. "This should never have happened."

"Why not?" she inquired innocently.

"Because you're still so young." Holding her by the shoulders, he moved her away slightly. "Don't you understand? I'm not the right man for you. The six years between us make a big difference. But even if we were the same age, I've had a much rougher life. You need someone as gentle and pure as yourself."

"Gentle? Pure? Good lord, you make me sound like some kind of face soap. I'm a human being, Julian. Maybe not a full-grown woman yet, but certainly well on the way to it. The last thing I want is to be put up on a pedestal."

He smiled crookedly. "I'm afraid that is not at all where I want to put you, but never mind. Right now I'm getting you home to your parents. Then I have something to...take care of."

Arlette hadn't asked what. Having grown up among Cajun men, she knew perfectly well what Julian intended to do. She simply saw no reason to discuss it.

Her mother was still awake when they reached her house. Maria Dumas came down the stairs in her bathrobe, frowning slightly. "Julian . . . is everything all right?"

"Yes," he said quietly, his hand on Arlette's shoulder. "But I think you should be a little more careful in the future about who Arlette goes out with."

"I see," her mother said quietly, surveying her silent, flushed daughter. "We are very grateful to you, Julian."

"No need," he assured her. To Arlette he added, "I'll see you soon."

She nodded, not looking at him as he left. Her mother asked few questions, for which she was grateful. Maria simply ran a hot tub for her daughter, brought her a glass of milk, and sat with her until she fell asleep.

Several days later Arlette had learned that the boy she had been with that night had left town suddenly, after being involved in some sort of accident that left both his eyes blackened.

The following weekend she had gone out with Julian, and she had kept on doing so for the two years that she had remained in Arkady.

How much of that did he remember, she wondered as the car turned onto the narrow dirt road leading to her parents' home. The white clapboard house, set beside a copse of cypress trees near a meandering inlet, was old but lovingly cared for. Generations of Dumases had grown up there, stretching back to before the Civil War.

A large porch dotted by columns ran the width of the house. Above it, projecting over the entrance to shade the downstairs rooms, was the second floor. An outside stairway led up to a narrow veranda from which doors opened directly onto the bedrooms. The traditional Cajun arrangement allowed for both congeniality and privacy.

Louis was out of the truck with a bound and hurrying up the steps to the porch as Arlette and Julian followed somewhat more slowly. They could hear him calling to the family, telling them whom he'd brought home, and then the excited murmur of a woman's voice as Maria Dumas hurried out to greet him.

"Julian!" she exclaimed with a warm smile that lit up features very like her daughter's. "It is so good to see you. You've stayed away much too long."

"Too long," he agreed, giving her a big hug. "Especially since you're even prettier than ever."

She laughed at his flattery and tucked her arm into his. "Come on inside. Supper will be ready soon. While I'm getting it on the table you can tell me all about what you've been up to."

"Not *all*," he insisted teasingly as they disappeared through the door. "A man has to be allowed some secrets."

Arlette looked after them with mingled wistfulness and annoyance. She didn't blame her mother for liking Julian so much, but she could wish Maria hadn't made it so obvious. It was hard to be reminded that if her family had had its way, Julian would long since have become part of it.

"I knew Mom would be thrilled," Louis said, either unaware of his sister's mood or deliberately ignoring it. "She's always thought the world of Julian. Pa, too."

Arlette murmured something noncommittal and headed for the outside stairs. She wanted to shower

and change her clothes before confronting Julian
again. And she wanted time to think about how to
cope with his reappearance in her life.

The room she had slept in for the first eighteen years
of her life was set up under the eaves of the house.
Small and pleasantly furnished, it had been her sanc-
tuary from the world, her place to dream of a future
that had seemed at once frightening and enthralling.
The wallpaper with its tiny pink flowers was a little
worn now, and the braided rug beside the four-poster
bed had definitely seen better days, but she liked the
room just as it was.

The two suitcases she had brought with her from
New York stood next to the dresser. The day before
she had unpacked only what she needed immediately,
and she hadn't gotten around to doing more that
morning. Sorting through the clothes would have to
wait a little longer, since she wasn't about to give the
impression that she was deliberately avoiding Julian.

Selecting a blue cotton skirt and soft yellow blouse,
she took them with her to the bathroom across the
hall. After a quick shower she put on fresh makeup,
dressed, and stopped again in her room long enough
to splash on a few drops of a light floral fragrance.

It was growing dark as she went downstairs to join
the others. Their voices floated up the stairwell, full of
good humor and laughter. With them came the
mouth-watering aromas of her mother's cooking.
Wryly she thought that whatever else the evening
might hold, there would be no excuse for going hungry.

The family was gathered in the kitchen, which took
up the entire back of the house. Arlette's father, her
brother, and Julian sat at the oak table. Maria was at

the cast iron stove, stirring a pot of gumbo. Not far away was the large loom on which she wove the traditional Cajun cotton, grown in her backyard, following patterns handed down to her by her mother and her mother's mother and so on into the distant past.

"There you are, dear," she said as Arlette joined them. "We were wondering where you'd gone to."

"I needed to change. This weather's still a bit much for me." She smiled at her mother and gave her father a quick hug before going to the tall cherry armoire that held the dishes. She was beginning to take plates out to set the table when she heard the scrape of a chair and looked over her shoulder.

Julian had stood up and was coming toward her. "I'll give you a hand."

"Oh, no," she said hastily, grabbing the rest of the plates. "It's not necessary. Besides, you're a guest."

As she quickly began to set the table, he shrugged and sat down again. "Let her do it," Louis advised with a grin. "She's just trying to show you how domestic she is."

Arlette's normally soft mouth tightened ominously, prompting her father to chuckle. Charlie Dumas was a big, lanky man with the raw-boned strength that came only from a lifetime of hard, physical work. In addition to the oystering that provided most of the family's income, he also farmed and hunted, thinking nothing of regularly working twelve hours a day and longer. His chiseled features were weathered to the consistency of old leather against which his blue eyes shone brightly.

"Easy there," he said to Louis. "Another minute and there'll be fur flying at this table. Arlette, honey, stop fussing and sit down."

Julian caught her eye and smiled. He held out the chair beside him. "Your dad's right, honey. Sit down."

Not for a moment did she mistake the endearment for anything other than what it was intended to be: a deliberate taunt. He was reminding her, none too gently, that if she didn't want to upset her family, she wouldn't let them discover how uncomfortable she was around him.

"Whatever you say," she murmured with a frosty smile as she slid into her seat. Taking a deep breath, she struggled to relax.

Julian was, after all, only a man. Better looking than most, but really not all that special. She knew dozens of men in New York who were more urbane, and certainly more charming, than this hard-edged oil rig worker in the worn workshirt and frayed chinos.

If she could just remember that, maybe she would be all right.

"Arlette, you haven't even tasted your gumbo," her mother broke in softly.

Abruptly aware that the others at the table were looking at her with expressions ranging from puzzled to amused, Arlette hastily picked up her spoon. The thick stew of pork, shrimp, okra and other local specialities was delicious as always. She took another spoonful and resolved not to let Julian spoil her appetite.

"Will you be staying long?" her father asked after they had brought him up-to-date on the latest news around town. That was easy enough, since there wasn't much.

"It's hard to say," Julian told him. "I'm looking for a house to buy."

"That's good to hear," Maria said. "We'd love to have you nearby."

They smiled at each other warmly. Arlette smothered a sigh and made a concerted effort to be polite. "What kind of house are you interested in?" she asked dutifully.

"Nothing too big. Eight to ten rooms would be enough, on a good size piece of land, say thirty to forty acres."

Thinking that he must be kidding, since no oil rig worker could afford such a spread, Arlette started to laugh, only to break off when she realized that her family were all nodding understandingly.

"The Beaufort place is still on the market," Louis said. "Maybe you ought to take a look at it."

"Imagine Julian buying that," Maria said. "Wouldn't tongues wag around here then."

"Wag right off," Charlie laughed. "The place would suit you, too, Julian. Be fine for entertaining and all that other stuff big time oil men are supposed to do."

Big time oil men, Arlette repeated to herself. What on earth were they talking about? Tentatively, she asked, "Isn't the Beaufort property very expensive?"

Julian shrugged and reached for his beer. "Probably, but what isn't these days? You get what you pay for."

She stared at him in bewilderment, but he merely gazed back mildly, as though knowing of no reason why she should be perplexed.

After a moment her mother said, "Of course, there's always the Larouse spread. I remember seeing that house when I was a girl. It looked like a palace then, and I'll bet it could again."

"I'll keep that one in mind," Julian assured her. "Although I have to admit I'm not too anxious to tromp through house after house on my own. It gets tedious after a while."

"It wouldn't if you had company," Maria said. As though the idea had only just occurred to her, she said, "Arlette, why don't you go along with Julian and help him out? A man can always use a woman's advice when he's thinking of settling down."

Making a mental note to have a talk with her mother, Arlette murmured, "I'm sure Julian wouldn't want me tagging after him. Besides, I have some things I need to do myself."

"You're going to be at loose ends till you line up interviews," her father reminded her, apparently intending to be helpful. "As for tagging along, I'm sure Julian wouldn't mind, would you?" He looked at their guest encouragingly.

Julian shot her a lazy smile as he shook his head. "Of course not. Why, I can remember a time when if I looked over my shoulder and didn't see Arlette, I worried something had happened to her."

The family thought that was quite amusing; they chuckled appreciatively. Arlette did not. She didn't like being reminded of the period in her life when she had been so utterly dependent on Julian, especially not when she remembered where that dependency had led.

As lightly as she could manage she said, "Isn't it fortunate that we all grow up eventually."

Something flickered behind his hazel eyes that looked almost like admiration tinged with regret. "You certainly did," he said softly. "The pretty young girl I used to know turned into a lovely woman."

"What a sweet thing to say, Julian," Maria exclaimed when her daughter made no comment.

He shook himself slightly, as though suddenly remembering that he and Arlette were not alone. With another of the cool smiles she was already beginning to realize masked deep feelings, he said, "I meant it. No one could ask for better company while house hunting." Turning slightly, he addressed her directly. "Busy as you are, I'd still appreciate it very much if you'd join me."

He spoke so unassumingly, almost with a touch of diffidence, that Arlette was taken aback. The Julian she remembered had barely known how to ask for anything; he had simply assumed that what he wanted was his to take by right.

Or at least that was how he had seemed to her at the time. With the benefit of hindsight, she could better understand that the young man reared in poverty and looked down on by many in the community might not have been confident enough to risk rejection.

He was certainly doing so now. She had only to say no, she was too busy, her job hunt would take all her time, or even simply that she didn't want to. Her family would be puzzled, perhaps even a little hurt, but they would hardly force her to be with him. For all their fondness for Julian, she was still their daughter and came first with them.

Who did Julian come first with, she wondered unwillingly. Was there a special woman in his life who placed him above all else? A stab of pain darted through her.

She knew all too well what it felt like to care for him in such a way. And she knew how that caring had led to pain. Having been down that road once, surely she wouldn't be tempted to walk it again.

There was only one way to convince herself—and him—of that. "I'll be happy to go house hunting with you," she said calmly. "Just don't expect me to be an expert. Apartments are more my speed."

"We'll learn together," he assured her.

If they did, it would be the first time.

He stayed several hours more, playing checkers with Charlie after supper and talking with Louis about conditions in the oil fields. "Finding a job is tough right now," he acknowledged as he accepted a cup of chicory-flavored coffee from Maria. "Since prices dropped, all the major companies have laid off workers. But that's starting to change. For instance, Petrex will be hiring soon."

"Are you sure?" Arlette asked. She followed the oil business closely enough to know that Petrex was a company that had fallen on hard times. Its management seemed to lack whatever was necessary to bring it back to prosperity.

"It's a safe bet," Julian told her, making her wonder how he came by such inside information. She added that to the list of questions she wanted to ask him, a list that was growing steadily.

He and Charlie had one more game of checkers, which Julian narrowly lost, before he stood up, stretched, and prepared to take his leave. "Thanks for the best meal I've had since the last time I was here," he told Maria sincerely.

"Don't you dare be a stranger any longer," she admonished him with a smile.

He assured her that he wouldn't and said goodnight, after politely refusing Louis's offer of a ride. "It's a nice night. . . . I'll enjoy the walk." Turning to Arlette, he asked, "Keep me company as far as the gate?"

Mainly because she could think of no reason not to, she agreed. "Don't hurry back, honey," her mother called after them. "I'll finish the washing up and leave the door unlocked."

"No one could ever accuse my family of being subtle," Arlette said wryly as she walked down the porch steps beside Julian.

"They mean well."

"I know. It's just . . . embarrassing."

He stopped in the shadows beneath the old cypress tree. There was no moon, only starlight, but it was enough for her to see his face. "Why?" he asked.

She looked away for an instant, then looked back and caught his gaze. "I keep thinking about what might have been," she admitted finally. "They would have been so happy."

"I never knew for sure, but I guessed you didn't tell them I'd asked you to marry me."

"It was cowardly, I admit. But it was hard enough to tell them that I was leaving without adding that."

He sighed softly and looked away into the darkness. "I was so angry. For months I couldn't think of you without cursing."

"I blamed you, too," she murmured. "I kept thinking that if you'd only been more understanding, more tolerant, things would have worked out."

"You wanted to leave," he reminded her, "to go to college and build a career for yourself. I wanted you to stay, to be my wife and have my children. There wasn't much room for compromise between those two positions."

"No," she admitted, "I suppose not. If I'd stayed, we both would have been stuck with less than either of us deserved."

His dark brows drew together slightly. "Do you really believe that?"

Arlette nodded. "I would always have regretted not having the courage to leave and try to fulfill my dreams, and you would have had a wife who wasn't fully committed to that role. We both would have suffered."

He took a step closer to her, his hand smoothing away an errant strand of her chestnut hair in a gesture remembered from long ago. "This new role of yours— geologist—is it everything you hoped?"

She stared straight ahead, her eyes focused on the breadth of his chest. Beneath the workshirt, worn thin by uncountable washings, she could see the steady rise and fall of his breathing and imagined that it increased a little. "Is anything ever?"

He laughed faintly, deep in his throat, where the buttons of the shirt were open and the dark springiness of ebony curls showed. "It sounds as though life in the big city has made you cynical."

"No, not that. Only cautious."

His blunt-tipped fingers stole under her chin. Gently but insistently, he lifted her head until their eyes met. "What part of you has become cautious, Arlette? Your mind . . . your spirit . . . or is it your heart?"

"All of me," she murmured, her throat suddenly tight. His square jaw was shadowed by a day's growth of beard. She thought of the times he had teased her about how sensitive her skin was, and because of it had shaved both morning and evening.

A memory surfaced deep in the recesses of her mind, an image of herself perched on the rickety counter in the bathroom of the mobile home where he had lived after moving out of his parents' place.

She could see him standing before her, younger than he was now, but otherwise not much different. A towel was wrapped around his taut waist; except for that he was naked. Creamy white shaving foam covered his lean cheeks. She had watched, fascinated, as he stroked away swath after swath of it until at last his face was again revealed to her.

That mundane activity had been special to her because of its very ordinariness. She had easily envisioned herself watching him do exactly the same thing ten or twenty years from then. Until she had fully realized what truly becoming part of his life would mean.

"I have to live in myself, Julian," she said softly. "Not through someone else. That's what you couldn't understand."

His thumb caressed the fullness of her lower lip slowly, as though tracing the pattern of his own thoughts. "I was offering you everything I had. It hurt that it wasn't enough."

"You couldn't give me myself," she murmured. The tightness in her throat had spread downward, and she was having trouble remembering to breathe. "Only I could do that."

"And have you?" he whispered as his dark head lowered.

She opened her mouth to answer, knowing as she did so that she had no idea what her response would be. But before she could even attempt it, Julian's arms closed around her. The tensile power of his embrace made her gasp softly even as his lips claimed hers.

Three

——

Julian had meant the kiss as a way of proving to himself that his feelings for Arlette had changed, that she no longer had the effect on him that she once had. What he discovered instead was that the passage of years had only made her even more intensely desirable to him.

The softness of her mouth beneath his, the warmth of her slender body, the special womanly fragrance he had always associated uniquely with her, all combined to make him forget everything except the need to make her share his feelings. No matter what else happened, he could not afford to let her stand apart from him, aloof and untouchable.

As he parted her lips further, he felt the shudder that ran through her and tightened his arms. Deep within him was the fear that if he gave her the slightest chance she would flee from him, as she had once before.

But Arlette was not thinking of flight; in fact, she wasn't thinking at all. The passion Julian evoked made it impossible for her to do anything except feel.

Instinctively she arched against him, her arms twining around his neck as her fingers combed through his thick black hair. The unyielding muscles of his chest pressed against her breasts, reminding her vividly of the differences between them. He was all driving strength and thrusting demand, at once the perfect match to her womanly softness, and its completion.

She trembled as his big work-hardened hands stroked down her back and came to settle finally on the slim curves of her hips. He murmured her name huskily as he drew her even closer, making her vividly aware of how much he wanted her.

"Arlette...you're a fever in my blood...like the hot summer wind whispering through the bayous. No matter how far I've gotten from you, I still hear you calling to me."

She wanted to tell him that he was not alone in his affliction; the hot wind called to her, as well. She sensed its whispering deep within her and knew the meaning of its urgings.

They would be so easy to give in to. Every womanly instinct she possessed told her that all she had to do was acquiesce and Julian would do the rest.

The moonless night sheltered them. They were completely alone in a setting of primitive beauty. What could be more natural than to yield to the cravings of their bodies?

Except that after the star-filled night would come the dawn, and with it regret. On the verge of a new life that would see the fulfillment of all she had worked for and dreamed of, she could not afford to go back. The past was a closed book, best left undisturbed.

Gently at first, then with increasing firmness when he resisted, she drew away from him. "We can't Julian. Whatever we shared is over. We're different people now."

Reluctantly he let her pull back, but kept his hands on her hips. "You're so sure of that?"

She wasn't, but despite that she nodded. "I'd like for us to be friends, if we can manage that. Anything else is too threatening."

A wry smile curved the mouth that moments before had so sweetly tormented her. "Friends? Do you really believe that's possible for us?"

Her soft mouth set in a stubborn line he remembered all too well. Her hands remained pressed against his chest, her arms braced. She would not give an inch, simply because she could not afford to.

"I'm not going to mince words with you, Julian. Much as I'd like to believe that I've become immune to you, what just happened proves that isn't the case. I'm simply not willing to run the risk of getting involved with you again."

His hands fell away from her, and she stepped back quickly. He continued to smile, but his eyes were watchful. "Yet you're willing to be friends?"

Softly, she said, "I'm willing to try."

He continued to study her for a moment, then shrugged his broad shoulders. "All right, friend. I'll pick you up around ten tomorrow morning. The real estate agent gave me a list of houses a yard long. Let's see how many of them we can get through."

She agreed, relieved that the encounter had ended so amicably, yet also a little surprised. The Julian she had known would never have given in so readily.

A short while later she went back inside. Lying in bed that night, she tried hard to reassure herself that seeing him again wasn't a mistake. Surely they were capable of being friends. The thought that not even that might be possible for them filled her with such sadness that she determinedly pushed it aside.

Her dreams that night were vivid and stormy, filled with the murmurings of a hot wind. She woke the next morning glad that she had no clear memory of them.

After breakfast, Arlette made several calls to the firms that had responded to her letters. She was able to set up two interviews for the next day, both in New Orleans. The prospect of shortly finding a job excited her. At least until she glanced out the window and saw Julian driving up.

The low-slung black sports car he parked in front of the house was only slightly less surprising than Julian himself. She had never before seen him dressed in such elegant and obviously expensive clothes.

Perfectly tailored black slacks accentuated his narrow hips and long, powerful legs. The white silk shirt tucked into them looked as though it had been made for him. He moved gracefully, clearly perfectly at ease with the accoutrements of wealth.

Glad that she had taken the time that morning to unpack a buttery soft suede skirt and handknit cotton sweater, she went quickly down the steps to join him. "Nice car," she said, inclining her head toward it. "Have you had it long?"

His gaze wandered over her briefly before he responded. "A few months. It handles well."

"Which, of course, is the only reason you bought it," she said with a gentle smile.

He laughed and opened the car door for her. "Actually, my reasons had more to do with self-indulgence than practicality. I'd always wanted one of these."

Arlette could see why. Sinking into the leather seat, she had the sensation of being enveloped in luxury. The rich fragrance of the upholstery combined with the patina of the mahogany dashboard and the impressive array of dials and gauges made her think wryly of her own beaten-up Mini. To call both those vehicles cars was to suggest that a weed was the same as a rose.

Julian slid in behind the wheel and turned the ignition key. The powerful engine roared to life. As he adroitly maneuvered the car down the narrow road she watched him surreptitiously. Once again she was struck by how at ease he was, as though he had always been surrounded by such affluence when, in fact, she knew he had been anything but.

"I'm trying to think of a tactful way to ask you something," she said at length, "but I can't seem to come up with one, so I may as well just blurt it out. Where on earth did you get so much money?"

He shot her a quick grin. "At least you're not afraid to speak your mind. I meet plenty of people who wonder about the source of my wealth but don't have the nerve to ask me."

"Nerve is something I always had in ample supply," she admitted wryly. "But if I'm being rude, just say so. I know your finances are none of my business."

"I don't mind," he assured her. "Besides, there's nothing complicated about how I came by the money.

After I left Arkady I knocked around on the rigs in the Gulf, later up by Alaska, and finally over in Saudi Arabia. I met a lot of useful people, some of whom agreed to stake me when I decided to try my hand at wildcatting. The first couple of wells I drilled brought nothing but dust, but the third hit big and I haven't looked back since.''

Arlette nodded thoughtfully. It made sense that he had become a wildcatter. Such men were the lone wolves of the oil and gas business, the risk takers and daredevils who put their lives and fortunes on the line again and again.

Working without the backup of the giant energy companies, they relied on a combination of expertise, instinct and sheer luck to bring them out ahead. If they bet right, they became fabulously wealthy. If they didn't, more often than not they simply tried again.

"I'm glad for you," she said sincerely. "There's no one I know who deserves success more."

Julian shrugged a little self-consciously. He had looked forward to telling her of his achievements, and not for the most praiseworthy of motives. There lurked in him the need to make sure she knew exactly what she had given up when she refused to marry him. Now she did, and he found himself slightly ashamed of having made the point so obviously.

"It's nothing a lot of other people haven't done," he said. "You've achieved just as much in your own way."

"That's nice of you to say, but getting a degree in geology isn't quite the same as creating a very successful business. However," she added, "I do feel I'm headed in the right direction."

He had to agree with that. Years ago she had made up her mind about what she wanted, and it didn't seem that anything was going to stop her from achieving her objectives. Much as he might regret her decision, he couldn't help but admire the tenacity with which she had stuck to it.

Moments later they pulled off the main road onto the gravel driveway leading to the first house on Julian's list. Like so many others in the area, it had been built in the previous century for the family of a cotton grower, and had long since fallen into disrepair.

Arlette got out of the car slowly, her eyes on the house. Despite the decades of neglect, the graceful lines of the portico remained intact. Tall white columns rose to a peaked roof. Behind them, floor-to-ceiling windows glinted in the sun.

The scent of honeysuckle was heavy in the air, and off in the distance she could hear the drone of bees. A wistful feeling settled over her, partly regret for what had once been, but also a yearning to restore the lost beauty of that bygone time.

"How lovely this is," she said as they walked up the brick steps to the porch. "Imagine what it was like when people lived here. I can almost see the carriages coming and going with exquisite women in silk and lace ball gowns, and tall, handsome men in frock coats and breeches."

"Scarlett O'Hara and Rhett Butler?" he asked gently as he unlocked the double doors and eased them open. The smell of dust and old wood drifted toward them. It was dark inside, but they could make out the stately proportions of the entry hall and the wide marble staircase curving upward to the second floor.

"Let's get some of these shutters opened," Julian said. Moments later light flooded the hall, making Arlette raise a hand to shade her eyes.

When she lowered it and looked around slowly, a soft sigh escaped her. "It's perfect. Everything about it is exactly right."

She was referring to the harmonious grouping of the black-and-white tiled floor, the high walls with their graceful moldings, and the ceiling decorated with what had clearly once been a magnificent mural of gods and goddesses at play. But Julian took a more mundane view.

"It's great if you like dry rot, spider webs and what look very much like bat droppings," he said with a grin.

"Mere details. Nothing that couldn't be taken care of." Glancing at an opened set of doors toward the east, she added eagerly, "Let's see what's over there."

They walked into what had once been the dining room. French doors looked out at a spacious garden complete with a large stone fountain. Opposite the doors was an immense marble-mantled fireplace. Above where the dining table must have been was a crystal chandelier, still beautiful even with a covering of dust.

Despite his earlier comment, Julian glanced around appreciatively. "They really did know how to do things back then. Everything in proportion, and everything with a purpose, if only to please the senses."

As he spoke, he reached out and took her hand, smiling down at her. Their gazes held for a moment before he said, "Come on. Let's see what else there is."

Together they explored the rest of the house, discovering a parlor, reception room and office on the first floor. Upstairs were five bedrooms with baths.

The plumbing looked as though it had been added in stages over several decades; all of it was in need of repair, if not replacement. There was a gaping hole in the floor outside one of the bedrooms, along with further evidence that the house had not been completely unoccupied in the years since its owners had moved out.

"Hobos have been here," Julian said as he nodded toward a small pile of empty tins in a corner of the master suite.

"They don't seem to have done any damage."

"How can you tell?" he asked wryly. "I'm not sure this place isn't about to fall down."

"A structural engineer could reassure you about that," Arlette hastened to remind him. "But remember, these places were built to last centuries."

"You really like it," he said softly.

The warmth of his tone made her uncomfortable. She was abruptly aware that her hand was still nestled in his. Anyone coming upon them suddenly would have to be pardoned for thinking they were a married couple inspecting what might be their new home.

That impression was further reinforced when she caught sight of them in the tall gilt mirror propped against one wall. A lighter space on the wall above it showed where it had once hung. The glass had long since become dim and speckled, but even so she could make out how they looked together.

Although she was of slightly more than medium height for a woman, beside Julian she looked small and rather delicate. The wide sweep of his shoulders and chest emphasized by contrast the slenderness of her own form. The slight tan she had acquired in the last few days seemed pale beside the weathered darkness of his skin.

For all that he was now an extremely successful executive, he was also a man accustomed to long hours of grueling work outside in all kinds of climates. The strength of his body and the chiseled quality of his features testified to that. There was nothing in the least soft or yielding about him, yet he was capable of great gentleness. She knew that all too well.

"Perhaps we should go on," she suggested. "There must be other houses you want to see."

"I suppose...." His deep voice trailed off. He, too, was looking in the mirror, not at himself but at the woman beside him. In some ways she was very much as he remembered her, lovely, desirable, feminine in the best sense of the word.

Yet he could hardly ignore how much she had changed. There was a strength and confidence about her that he had not seen before. With a small spurt of surprise he realized that even as he had been coming into his own as a man, she had been doing much the same as a woman.

The results were enticing enough to make him at least a little less resentful of her hard-won independence.

They left the house through the back door and walked through the garden. Much of it had long since reverted to the wild, but they could still make out azalea and rose bushes that must have been lovingly cared for in some distant time.

The stone fountain was clogged with leaves and other debris, but looked as though it might be fairly easy to clear. Nearby a broad swath of lawn ran down toward the river. Several small boats drifted past, their sails glinting in the sunlight.

"I could get used to this place," Julian admitted as he opened the car door for her again. "It grows on you."

She nodded quickly. "The house does need a lot of fixing up, but the results could be spectacular."

"I'll keep it in mind," he promised as he switched on the engine. "Let's see now, that's one down and thirty-seven to go."

"Thirty-seven?" Surely there couldn't be that many houses he wanted to see.

His hazel eyes gleamed with amusement. "Well, maybe fewer than that, but I want to do a thorough job of this."

"I remember when you bought your first car," Arlette said resignedly. "That second-hand Buick that looked as though it had been through a war, on the losing side. How many lots did we tromp through before you settled on it?"

"I lost count. You were very good about keeping me company."

She wasn't about to remind him that back then she would have gone just about anywhere and done just about anything to be with him. Instead she murmured, "I learned a lot about cars in the process."

"That Buick was a gem. Probably the best car anyone ever got for two hundred bucks."

"What happened to it?" she asked.

"I sold it two years later to a guy from Shreveport. Got five hundred for it."

Arlette laughed and shook her head. "Always the wheeler-dealer. Was there ever something you didn't make a profit on?"

His smile faded as he cast her a speaking glance. She sighed and wished the question could be withdrawn.

They drove in silence the rest of the way to the second house.

"I don't know about you," Julian said some six hours later as they climbed back into the car yet again, "but I've about had it. How many does that make?"

"Twelve," Arlette said, checking off the list. "And I feel the same way. After a while, they all start to look alike."

"You've seen one run-down antebellum mansion, you've seen them all?"

"I suppose. Anyway, my feet are about to go on strike."

"Do you still like to have them rubbed?" he asked innocently as they got back on the road. At Arlette's blush, he chuckled. "Sorry, but I couldn't resist. How about letting me buy you supper to make up for it?"

She hesitated, thinking that it really wasn't prudent to be with him much more than she already had been. Still, she was hungry and didn't want to seem ungracious.

"All right, but if you wouldn't mind, I'd prefer to keep it simple. Much more of Mom's cooking and I'm not going to fit into my clothes."

"I could say something about your not having to worry about that, but it might sound too personal."

"That's okay," she assured him with a smile. "Friends are allowed to reassure each other."

"You'll have to fill me in on what else friends can do," Julian said after they were seated at a table toward the back of the restaurant he had suggested.

Five miles outside of Arkady, Janine's Place had a well-deserved reputation for good food and friendly service. Arlette hadn't been there in years and was glad he had thought of it.

"I'm sure you know as much about that as I do," she said. "What do you do when you get together with the guys?"

"It's been a while since I had time for that, but let me see what I can remember.... We used to play cards, drink beer, chase girls and raise hell." The corners of his mouth quirked upward in a wry smile. "Any of that appeal to you?"

"Can't say it does. I guess what you're telling me is that men and women don't have much experience being friends."

"That's about the size of it, and if you tell me how many great male friends you left back in New York, I'm going to be a little ticked off."

"Only a little?" she asked with a smile. Before he could answer she went on hastily. "No, I'm not going to claim to have a lot of male friends. I think you're right about it being hard to keep friendship apart from any sort of romantic involvement. But it can be done. Look at how well some brothers and sisters get along. For all his kidding around, I consider Louis to be a very good friend."

"There's only one problem with that example," he said as the waitress arrived to take their orders. The menu, such as it was, was printed on a large chalkboard near the door.

"Crawfish, please," Arlette told the waitress.

"The same," Julian said. When the woman was gone and they were alone again, he added, "I don't happen to be your brother."

"I hardly need to be reminded of that," Arlette said, reaching for the basket of fresh-baked French bread the waitress had left. She automatically held it out to him before selecting a piece for herself. "But you were once a kind of brother to me, when I was growing up. If you're honest, I think you'll admit that back then you thought of me as a little sister."

It was true; he had. But later his feelings had changed. He could have pointed out to her that if she was honest, she'd admit that hers had, too. But that would only take them down a road she was clearly unwilling to walk.

"All right," he said at length. "I'll give it a try."

For the remainder of the meal they stayed with more neutral topics. "Tell me about the kind of job you're looking for," Julian urged.

Pleased that he was taking an interest, she said "Something that will really allow me to use my training. I'd like to work directly in the field, identifying new sources of oil and gas."

"In other words, in the riskiest part of the business." He smiled at her over the steaming plates of succulent pink crawfish the waitress had set before them. "I don't suppose you'd settle for a nice safe job in a lab?"

She wrinkled her nose. "No thanks. I've already been that route, and it's nothing short of boring. Exploration is where the action is in our business." It was also, though she didn't say so, the quickest route for advancement in the industry. A successful well meant not only a new source of energy but also raises and promotions for everyone involved in its development.

"You're ambitious," Julian said quietly, studying her from across the table. He didn't say it critically, but Arlette still felt defensive.

"I know there are people who think that's wrong for a woman," she said. "But I don't see why half the world's population should be denied the right to make the best use of their potential."

His eyebrows rose slightly. "Don't you think you're exaggerating? Women have made enormous strides in the last few years, and I'm sure they'll continue to do so, even though nobody has yet managed to solve a fundamental problem."

"What's that?" she asked.

"How to make up for the loss of women from the home. People are just beginning to realize that what they did there was very important. It seems as though we never really valued homemaking and child rearing until so many women stopped doing them."

Arlette thought of how much her mother had done to create the loving harmony of her own family and nodded slowly. "I see what you mean, but I still think it's wrong to try to confine women to those occupations."

"Of course it is, but this is hardly an ideal world. Women who are trying to have both careers and families are finding that out. They have a very tough time of it."

"Do you employ many women?" Arlette asked.

"About ten percent of my staff is female. But none of them are in supervisory or management positions. They work mainly as secretaries, although there are a few women on rig crews."

"Don't you think that's unfair?"

"It's not my choice; if a qualified woman comes along, I'll hire her. But the women working for me now are doing so to help support their families. In some cases they're the sole support. They don't have the freedom to devote themselves to a career."

Arlette couldn't really argue with him about that, though she would have liked to. He was right about the situation of many women in the work force; in fact, she was surprised by his understanding of the issues.

"I still say," she said, "that it should be possible to have both a career and a family. And it would be, if employers were more supportive. Instead of expecting women to behave exactly like men, they should encourage them to be themselves."

"Very laudatory, but not too realistic when you're worrying about keeping a business going."

They went on in that vein until the last of the crawfish was gone. Neither convinced the other, but that didn't seem to matter. What counted far more, at least with Arlette, was that they had spent an evening together without her thinking constantly of what they had once shared.

She was at once relieved by that, yet also faintly saddened. Lying in bed later that night, listening to the hum of the cicadas in the cypress trees, she tried to tell herself that it was best to forget the past and concentrate strictly on the future.

But she feel asleep before she was truly convinced.

Four

―――――

It was raining the next morning when Arlette woke up, the heavy bayou rain that fell in curtains from the leaden sky, coursed in rivulets off the drooping trees and ran in impromptu streams over the glistening roads.

Peering out the window, she smothered a sigh. Job interviews were tough enough without also having to battle lousy weather. Resigned to what promised to be a difficult day, she showered and dressed before going downstairs to join the family for breakfast.

Louis grinned admiringly when he saw her. "Is that one of those 'dress for success' suits, Sis?"

"I guess so," she admitted as she smoothed the navy blue linen skirt that matched her austerely tailored jacket. With it she wore a high-necked white blouse lacking even the hint of a frill. Her chestnut hair was pinned up in a discreet chignon, and she wore only the subtlest hint of makeup.

The effect was appropriately professional even though nothing could dim the innately feminine grace of her face and figure.

"You look just fine, honey," her mother assured her. "Now eat your breakfast. You'll need it today."

Arlette did as she was told. She joined a little in the conversation going on around the table, but her thoughts were on the interviews she would be having, and her family respected that.

As she was getting ready to leave, her father said, "Don't worry, sweetheart, they'll love you."

"Anyone who didn't would be too stupid to work for anyway," her mother added loyally.

Arlette laughed and kissed them both, then got an umbrella from the hall closet. Outside the rain was still streaming down. The gravel driveway was awash with runoff, but by running lightly across the grass she managed to reach her car without getting her shoes too muddy.

Going over in her mind the best route to take, she turned the key in the ignition. Nothing happened. She tried again with the same result. The third time it dawned on her that she really had a problem.

Getting out of the car with a muttered exclamation of disgust, she opened the umbrella and ran for the barn, where her brother was working on his beloved truck.

"Louis," she called, "could you come and take a look at my car? Something seems to be wrong with it."

"Sure, Sis." He walked back with her, propped open the hood and peered at the engine. Arlette stared at it dubiously. She had only the faintest notion of what the various parts were for.

After a few moments Louis straightened and shook his head. "Bad news. The fan belt's shot. You know that happens sometimes on rentals."

"Can you replace it?" she asked anxiously.

"Eventually, but I'll have to get the part first. Probably take a day or two."

"Oh, no! I've got to be in New Orleans in a couple of hours."

"Well, let's see now, you could take the truck, 'cept she's acting up and I'm not sure how far you'd get. Maybe Dad could lend you the Jeep."

"You know I never learned to drive a stick shift."

"Oh, yeah, that's right," he scratched his head thoughtfully. "Gosh, Sis, I don't know what to tell you. There's no place in Arkady to rent another car, and the bus doesn't run today."

"I suppose I'll have to call and tell them I can't make it," she said reluctantly. "That won't make a very good impression."

Louis shrugged sympathetically, but could offer no alternative. Arlette was turning toward the house when the sound of a car pulling up made her look back.

"Morning," Julian called. "Looks like you're off to the city."

"I was, until my car decided not to work," she told him glumly. "It couldn't have happened at a worse time, either. I've got two job interviews."

"Hop in then. I'll drive you."

"All the way to New Orleans? I couldn't ask you to do that; it's too far."

"I've got business there that I can take care of to-day as easily as some other time," he assured her, leaning over to open the passenger door. "Besides," he added as she hesitated, "what are friends for if they can't help you out of a tight spot?"

She could hardly disagree with that. "I really appreciate this." Getting into the car, she noticed Julian and Louis exchanging a quick grin, but thought nothing more of it. Moments later they were out on the road, heading toward the interstate.

The powerful car ate up the miles as she and Julian chatted amicably. "Tell me about these companies you're seeing today," he urged. "Maybe I can give you some tips."

She complied, then listened carefully as he told her what he knew of the men she would be meeting, what particular problems their companies faced, and how they were hoping to solve them. By the time he had finished they were on the outskirts of New Orleans.

"How do you know so much?" she asked. "It's as though you've thoroughly checked out each firm."

"I suppose you could say I have," he acknowledged. Before she could pursue that any further, he stopped the car in front of the office building where her first interview was scheduled. "How about I meet you back here at five and we'll get a bite to eat before heading back to Arkady?"

She agreed and added, "Thanks for doing this. I was really stuck."

"It's nothing," he assured her, then reconsidered. "Well, maybe it's a little something." Very gently, he touched his mouth to hers. "For luck."

The taste of him was still on her lips as she entered the building and made her way to the personnel department. After filling out all the usual forms, she met with two men from the research and development division. They were both clearly impressed with her qualifications and spent a large part of their time with her describing the benefits of joining their company.

It was much the same at her next stop. Though she didn't kid herself that the right job was simply going to fall into her lap, she felt increasingly confident as the day progressed.

The only real problem she encountered was a tendency on the part of the men she talked with to try to convince her to work in the lab rather than in the field. She listened to them patiently, but made it clear that she felt best suited to be part of an exploration team.

The low-slung black sports car was waiting by the curb when she arrived back at the spot where Julian had dropped her off. He was leaning against the hood, absently watching the passersby, and she had a moment to study him unobserved.

His ebony hair ruffled in the slight breeze that also flattened his shirt against his broad chest. In profile, his features looked even more like those of a Roman gladiator, or perhaps a matador, the eyes watchful, the mouth sensual, strength and pride evident in the firm set of the chin. There was also a hint of the predator in the way he looked over the passing crowd, almost like a hawk that felt no great urge to hunt yet was still alert to the presence of prey.

A shiver ran through Arlette. She felt slightly ridiculous to be thinking of him in such terms, but could not help it. There was something about him that set him apart from all other men, a sense of his own worth, perhaps, and a steady confidence in his abilities, born not of arrogance but of experience. He made her feel at once infinitely safe yet challenged in a way she could barely comprehend.

Taking a deep breath, she steadied herself and pinned on a bright smile she hoped would mask her inner confusion. "Hi, I hope you haven't been waiting long."

"Not at all," he assured her, straightening away from the car. Hazel eyes studied her for a moment before he added, "It went well?"

She nodded. "Better than I'd hoped." With a slight laugh, she admitted, "But I still feel as though I've been put through a wringer."

He smiled understandingly as she got into the car. "Good food will take care of that, but perhaps you'd like to freshen up first?"

In the muggy New Orleans heat, she did feel as though she was wilting. "I'd love to, but where...?" she asked when he slid in beside her.

"I keep an apartment in the French Quarter."

While she was coming to terms with that, he headed the car away from the business district and toward the heart of the old city, where the vibrant, exotic character of antebellum New Orleans was still very much alive.

Away from the honky-tonk strip of Bourbon Street the quiet elegance of classic French and Spanish-style buildings, many well over a century old, still existed. Arlette had always found them entrancing, designed as they were to create a haven of privacy in the middle of a bustling city.

The building where Julian had his apartment was some four stories tall and painted in a traditional blend of pastels that made it appear as a soft smudge of color against the brilliantly blue sky.

Inside, beyond the fanciful grillwork gate, was a secluded courtyard crossed by gravel paths and dotted with beds of red, pink and white azaleas. Stone benches were set out at intervals around a fountain. The sounds of the street were muted by the babbling of water and the trilling of birds nesting under the eaves.

"How beautiful," Arlette murmured reverently. "It's like a world all its own."

"Just walking through here relaxes me," Julian said as they reached the heavy oak door leading to the stairs. "It's one of the reasons I bought the apartment."

Arlette quickly discovered what his other reasons might have been. Situated on the third and fourth floors of the building, the duplex he led her to was an island of subdued beauty and luxury. The cream-colored walls, parquet floors and high ceilings were the perfect setting for the comfortably unobtrusive furnishings.

She thoroughly approved of the simplicity with which the apartment was decorated, seeing in it a refuge from the complexity of the outside world. "I'd have a hard time staying away from here," she said as he hung her jacket in the coat closet, "if this was mine. Are you sure you really want to buy a house?"

"I think so, though I intend to keep this place. It's very convenient to my offices."

"So it's strictly practical?" she asked teasingly, just as she had about the car.

He laughed and shook his head. "No, I won't claim that this time, either." He stood aside to let her precede him into the sun-filled living room, then asked, "Can I get you a drink?"

"Something light would be nice. While you're doing that, where can I freshen up?"

He pointed her in the direction of the guest bath, which was down a short hallway and connected to a large bedroom. Across from it she caught a glimpse of what was obviously the master suite, but looked away hastily.

It had begun to dawn on her that coming to the apartment with Julian might not have been such a good idea. Not because she didn't trust him, but precisely because she did.

Mulling over the inconsistency of that, she splashed cold water on her face at the marble and gilt sink, patted her skin dry with a fluffy towel, and redid her makeup.

Looking at herself in the lighted mirror, she frowned. The outfit that had been so appropriate for interviews was far too stodgy for dinner with an extremely attractive man, even if he was only a friend.

On impulse, she let down her hair, brushed it vigorously and let it fall naturally to her shoulders. She also undid the top three pearl buttons on her blouse, took another look in the mirror and redid one of them. Satisfied, she went back to join Julian in the living room.

He was sitting on the couch with his long legs stretched out in front of him and a cold beer in his hand. A glass of white wine was set on the inlaid table nearby.

As she entered the room he rose and said, "That didn't take long. Most women I know need far more time to get ready for anything."

"Perhaps they have more to work with," she suggested with a faint touch of asperity. Being reminded that he was a man well acquainted with feminine habits did not delight her.

"I wouldn't say that," he told her as she sat and reached for her glass. He joined her on the couch. They were far enough apart not to be touching, yet Arlette was acutely conscious of his presence. She took a quick sip of the wine, hoping it would steady her nerves.

A bit awkwardly she said, "This is very good."

"Thank you," he replied gravely. "Now, would you mind telling me why being here is making you so nervous?"

"It's not," she said quickly, only to relent an instant later. "Well, maybe a little. But it's silly, so do me a favor and just ignore it."

"That's very hard to do," he told her. "I find that everything about you interests me a great deal."

"I don't see why," she said honestly. "It's not as though I'm a raving beauty, or even particularly sophisticated."

"If you're fishing for compliments..."

"I'm not," she hastened to assure him. "All I'm doing is being realistic. We shared something very special once, but it didn't work out, and we should both acknowledge that."

"You seem to think I'm trying to turn back the clock," he said, regarding her quietly, "when in fact I know that's impossible. We've both changed, probably more than most people in the same amount of time. I'm very interested in the way you are now. Is there something wrong with that?"

Slowly she shook her head. "No, I suppose not. The truth is I'm very curious about you, too. What you've accomplished is nothing short of remarkable. It takes a very special person to do what you've done.''

A slight flush spread across Julian's lean face, subsiding quickly as his customary self-control asserted itself. "I don't have any real sense of achieving anything remarkable," he said sincerely. "Not that I'm unaware of how far I've come, or ungrateful for what I have now. But my mind seems to always be on the future and the present, rather than the past.''

"I suspect most successful people are that way, but," she added, glancing around the beautiful apartment, "you have to admit this is a long way from that trailer you used to live in.''

"That's true, but the change in circumstances could be deceptive. I'm still the same person inside.''

Arlette took another sip of her wine and wondered why it almost sounded as though he was warning her.

They went to a small restaurant in the French Quarter that the tourists hadn't yet discovered. Seated at a quiet table in the back, they talked throughout the excellent dinner.

Julian told her more about how he had made the progression from oil rig worker to wildcatter. Though he made light of the difficulties he had faced, she didn't underestimate them. He had done more than his share of hard physical work, while also taking risks most men would not even consider. For him they had all paid off, and she could not help but be very glad.

At his urging she told him how the interviews had gone. He agreed that she was getting some pressure to change her career objectives, but cautioned her that it was to be expected.

"Men are still hesitant about sending women into the field," he said. "It's partly concern over how the essentially male crews will react to them, but there's also genuine reluctance to expose them to the dangers encountered there."

"I appreciate that, but it should be up to me to decide what kinds of chances I want to take."

"Theoretically, I agree with you," Julian said. "But in actual fact I'd be hesitant myself about sending a woman into that kind of situation. Field work is more than just dangerous; it's exhausting, dirty, and more often than not ends in disappointment. Men have a natural instinct to want to protect women from things like that."

"Which is fine if the woman wants to be protected, but suppose she doesn't? Then the man should stand aside and let her do what she believes is right for herself."

"Even if it means she gets hurt?"

"Even then," Arlette insisted. She spoke from the deepest conviction. In her opinion, no one had the right to control another person's life, not even for the best of motives.

"What if this hypothetical man and woman we're discussing happen to care for each other?" Julian asked as he refilled first her wine glass and then his own. The dry Pouilly Fuissé he had ordered went very well with their shrimp *étoufée*, the traditional Cajun dish smothered in a dark red-brown roux flavored with pepper, onion, basil and thyme.

"That's different." Her eyes met his across the table. "People in love have special responsibilities to each other."

Julian's mouth tightened. "I've always thought so."

"Responsibilities that work both ways. It seems to me that in the best relationships each person encourages the other to fulfill his or her potential."

"Which I didn't do when I asked you to marry me instead of going away to college?"

"I'm not criticizing you," she said softly, "and I'm especially not trying to dredge up the past. As you said earlier, it's the present and the future that matter. But what happened between us convinced me that people have to be very cautious in the commitments they make, otherwise they can end up being badly hurt."

His blunt-tipped fingers clasped the fragile stem of the wine glass as he swirled the golden liquid ruminatively. "Were you?"

"Hurt? Of course I was. Refusing you was the hardest thing I've ever done." All too vividly she remembered that last night they had shared, when Julian had asked her to become his wife.

His proposal had not come as a complete shock, but she had still been at a loss as to how to deal with it. In retrospect she could see that her response had been clumsy and might easily have appeared unfeeling. But it had been sparked by the panic she felt at opposing him and her fear that with very little effort he would convince her to do as he wanted.

"You knew I was planning to go to college," she reminded him gently. "I'd been talking of little else for the previous two years. When I asked you to wait, you refused."

"I couldn't see a four-year separation," he said. "At best, we would have had a part-time marriage, with all the strains that entails."

"Was that the only reason?" she asked gently.

He hesitated a moment, then shook his head. "No, it's true there was more involved. I was afraid that going to college would put you out of my reach."

"But you went yourself."

"Only part-time. Most of what I learned came from experience."

"That hasn't exactly held you back," she said with a smile. Not for a moment did she believe that Julian, as he was now, felt inadequate because he hadn't had as much formal education as some other people. But she could see how that might have bothered him eight years ago.

"True," he admitted wryly. "And to be fair, I wonder if I would have gotten as far as I have with a family to worry about. I certainly couldn't have taken some of the risks I have."

Arlette doubted that anything could really have prevented him from achieving his goals, but she appreciated the suggestion that everything had worked out for the best for both of them. It relieved her of the guilt she had been feeling as she remembered her rejection of him.

She glanced down at her plate, then up at him again. "Do you mind if I ask you something?" When he shook his head, she went on. "How is it that you haven't married?"

He raised an eyebrow. "What makes you think I haven't?"

That possibility hadn't occurred to her. Dismayed by her lack of foresight, she flushed. "I'm sorry; I shouldn't have presumed so much."

He sighed and reached for her hand across the table, capturing it gently. "As it happens, you're right. I've thought about marriage from time to time, but frankly I enjoy my freedom. The older I get the less anxious I am to make promises I may not be able to keep."

"Plenty of people don't worry about that. They just go ahead and get married."

"And end up divorced, or miserable. No," he said, shaking his head, "if I ever do marry, it will be forever, so I had better be very careful who I pick. Besides," he added with a smile, "the last time I proposed I didn't get very far. Maybe my technique needs work."

Arlette was willing to bet that, if anything, it had improved over the years, but she wasn't about to tell him so.

Instead she said, "I agree that marriage frequently doesn't last. That's one of the reasons I'm so wary of it myself."

"You haven't come close either?"

"No, I can't say I have." She hoped he wouldn't press for any details on that particular subject. To let him know that he had been the only man in her life would make her far too vulnerable.

They left the restaurant a short time later and strolled past Jackson Square toward the river. At that hour, when the last vestiges of daylight had long since fled, the Mississippi was a sluggish gray ribbon winding south toward its meeting with the Gulf. A few barges and fishing boats could be seen riding at anchor as their crews settled down for the night.

Near the river it was a little cooler, but the sultry heat still clung to them. After they had walked a dozen or so blocks Julian suggested a stop at one of the nearby coffee houses. Over cups of the fragrant chicory brew and *beignets* sprinkled with powdered sugar, they chatted about other places they had been.

"I like New York," Arlette said, "but it can be overpowering. Also, the winters seem to last forever."

"You used to complain about the cold if the temperature fell below fifty," he kidded her gently. "I can imagine how happy you must have been plowing through the slush with snow trickling down your collar."

She shivered delicately. "Don't remind me. I couldn't get back here quickly enough."

"Of course, you realize that if you do join an exploration team, you could be sent almost anywhere in the world. Alaska, for instance."

"I try not to think about it," Arlette said. "There's plenty to be done right here in the Gulf, or in the nearby states."

Julian nodded and reached for another of the feather-light doughnuts. "That's where I expect to be working for at least the next ten years."

"After you take over Petrex?"

The doughnut slipped from between his fingers as his head jerked back. "How on earth did you figure that out?"

Rather pleased with herself, she didn't mind telling him. "It was simple, really. The fact that you're very knowledgeable about a company known to be having severe management problems started me wondering. Then, when you indicated you planned to settle down, it occurred to me that you'd want a stable base from which to work. That would mean buying a company somewhere in this area. I threw in your obvious prosperity and, *voilà*, came up with the answer." Actually, there had also been a fair measure of luck involved, but she saw no reason to mention that.

Julian shook his head admiringly. "Remind me not to try to keep secrets from you."

"Then I'm right?"

He lowered his voice slightly. "As it happens, I am preparing to make a bid for Petrex. Naturally I'd appreciate your not mentioning that to anyone."

She could easily understand why. If word of his intentions got out, Petrex stock would climb steeply in cost and he would have to spend that much more to get control.

"I won't breathe a word," she said sincerely. Try though she did to maintain a properly solemn expression in the face of such news, she couldn't quite manage it. An irrepressible smile curved her mouth as she added, "This is very exciting."

"That's one word for it," Julian said with a grin. "Also complicated, frustrating, time-consuming, plus a few others I won't mention. Let's just say I'll be very relieved when it's all sewn up."

"Will that be soon?"

"It has to be. Something like this can't stay under wraps very long." He swallowed the last of his coffee before adding, "I'm looking to have everything signed, sealed and delivered within the next couple of weeks."

Which undoubtedly meant that he would be extremely busy and she would see relatively little of him. She was thinking about that as they left the coffee shop and began walking back toward his apartment.

Five

I suppose we should be getting back to Arkady," Julian said as he unlocked the door and stood aside for Arlette to enter. He had left a light on in the living room. It glowed warmly against the shadowy backdrop of the curtained windows.

"I suppose..." she replied, thinking of how sleepy the food and wine, added to the tension of the day, had made her. It was a two hour drive to her parents' home; they couldn't be there before midnight. She was willing to bet that with the pressures surrounding the Petrex takeover, Julian hadn't had an easy day either. Left to himself, he would undoubtedly stay right where he was.

"Would you care for anything before we get started?" he asked.

She stifled a yawn and shook her head. "No, thanks."

"You're tired?"

"I'm afraid so." Looking up at him, she asked, "How about you?"

"The same. I'll be glad to get home."

But he was there already, or at least he would be if he didn't have to drive her back to Arkady. "Look...I wouldn't want to give you the wrong impression, but it occurred to me that it's not very nice to expect you to drive back tonight."

"I'm not following you."

She flushed slightly. "It's just that I noticed you have a guest room, and I was thinking it might be more sensible for me to stay there. That is, if you wouldn't mind."

"Mind?" He repeated as though he could hardly believe what he was hearing. "No, of course I wouldn't mind. I would have suggested it myself except that I thought it might make you feel... uncomfortable."

Arlette laughed self-consciously. "We're both adults; surely we can be trusted to spend a night in the same apartment without doing anything...foolish."

"You don't think your parents would object?"

It was on the tip of her tongue to remind him that so far as her parents were concerned, he could do no wrong. Instead she said, "They know I'm not a child anymore. We've both had a tough day, and we're both tired; what could be more natural than for us to stay here?"

"When you put it that way..."

"It's settled, then. If you'll show me where the linens are, I'll make up the bed."

"I think my housekeeper's already done that. But if there's anything else you need...?"

"Just a good night's sleep," she said as she turned toward the hall that led to the guest room. She was moving more quickly than she normally would have and hoped he wouldn't take that to mean she was nervous. She wasn't at all. Well, certainly no more than a little.

Julian was still standing in the foyer looking after her when she said good-night and closed the guest room door. Once inside, she managed to relax enough to marvel at her own boldness. Not, of course, that there was anything really daring about what she had done. They were simply being sensible.

As she removed her clothes and hung them away neatly in the closet, she reminded herself of that several times. In the bathroom cabinet she found spare toothbrushes still in their cellophane wrappers, as well as toothpaste and soap.

After taking care of her ablutions for the night, she padded back into the bedroom wrapped in an oversized towel that made her less aware of her lack of a nightgown or robe.

The bed was kingsize, with a firm mattress, large, fluffy pillows, and crisp white sheets that smelled like sunshine. She let the towel drop to the floor, then slipped between the sheets gratefully.

No sooner had she stretched out fully than she became aware of myriad small aches and pains throughout her body, the result of too much tension. She stretched luxuriously and promised herself a long bath in the morning.

But first, sleep beckoned. With the bedside lamp switched off, the room was comfortably dark. As her eyes adjusted she could make out the shapes of the simple but beautifully made dresser and table beyond the foot of the bed, and could see the soft rippling of the curtains at the floor-to-ceiling windows.

Muted sounds reached her: the distant hum of traffic along Bourbon Street; the soft coo of a bird in the garden below; the measured tread of footsteps that paused for a moment outside her door, then moved on. Another door nearby closed. She guessed it was the one to Julian's room and that he had now retired.

Her eyes fluttered shut as she turned over on her side and burrowed down further into the bed. A warm sense of contentment filled her. She drifted on it, smiling faintly, as consciousness dissolved.

Late in the night Arlette awoke. She had no idea at first what had disturbed her rest; several moments passed before she recognized the cause.

Rain was lashing against the partially opened windows. The curtains, which earlier had fluttered gently, streamed into the room on damp currents of air. Even as she sat up, clutching the covers to her, a finger of lightning ripped the sky open and illuminated the room in a ghostly glow. Hard on the lightning came a long, deep roll of thunder that seemed to shake the building to its very foundations.

Though she had been through numerous such storms, Arlette had never learned to enjoy them as some did. She found the sudden turmoil of nature frightening no matter how hard she tried to convince herself otherwise.

Her slender arm reached out from beneath the covers and fumbled for the switch on the lamp. She turned it once, twice, before realizing that the electricity must be out. For a moment she lay in bed, wondering what to do, before another bolt of lightning abruptly made the decision for her.

Scrambling out of the bed, she reached for the towel and was in the process of wrapping it around herself when the bedroom door opened.

Julian stood there, wearing a black silk dressing gown, his ebony hair rumpled and his jaw set. He also carried a flashlight, turned on but pointed at the floor.

"I'm sorry," he said quickly when she looked up, startled by his sudden entry. "I thought there might be some chance you were still asleep, and I didn't want to risk waking you."

"The storm took care of that," she assured him with a shaky laugh. Tucking the end of the towel firmly between her breasts, she gestured vaguely toward the window. "It seems like a bad one."

"No worse than usual. You've been through this before."

"Sure...it's no problem." Her voice trembled slightly.

"How about a brandy?" he suggested gently.

"Only if you'll join me," she said, embarrassed that he should think her afraid.

Together they walked down the hall toward the living room, Julian going first with the flashlight. "All the power is out," he said.

"I know. I tried to turn the lamp on. Do you have any idea when it'll come back on?"

"That's hard to say. It could be minutes, or hours. We'll just have to wait it out."

Arlette had known that before he spoke, but still wished it wasn't so. She sat down awkwardly on the couch, her arms wrapped around herself, as he went over to the bar.

He returned with two crystal snifters, each about a third full of amber liquid. "Here, this will make you feel better."

She took a sip, feeling it burn all the way down her throat, and made a face. "I suppose it grows on you."

He looked at her for a moment, then laughed. "It had damn well better. That stuff is older than you, sweetheart. It's considered very choice."

"Actually, it isn't bad," she admitted after another sip. "And it does make me feel warmer." With the storm had come a sudden lowering of the temperature. The sultry heat of a few hours before was gone, replaced by cool, damp air that chilled her bare arms.

"Here," Julian said as he put down his snifter and began undoing the belt of his robe, "take this."

"Oh, no," she assured him hastily. "I couldn't."

He ignored her protestations and stood up, removing the robe and draping it over her slender shoulders. She breathed a quick sigh of relief when she realized that he was wearing pajama bottoms. Of course, the fact that the top had apparently become lost somewhere didn't do all that much for her equilibrium.

Her gaze was drawn irresistibly to his bare torso. He was lean in the sense of not carrying an ounce of fat, but also broad and heavily muscled in a way more sedentary men could not hope to be. The graceful curve of his wide shoulders flowed down into a chest and arms fashioned by a master sculptor. Beneath his flat male nipples and along the clearly delineated line of his ribs were sheets of corded muscle. Thick black hair spread across the upper part of his chest before tapering in a line across his flat abdomen to vanish beneath the waistband of his pajamas. His skin was burnished to the shade of old whiskey; she caught herself wondering if he looked like that all over.

"Something wrong?" Julian asked as he noticed the slow flush spreading over her cheeks.

"Must be the brandy," she told him hurriedly. "I'm not used to it."

"You don't have to drink it if you don't want to, but I do think it would help."

As he spoke a further peal of thunder shook the room. Arlette jumped slightly and took another sip. She swallowed too much and coughed, but quickly regained control of herself. "Are you sure you aren't cold?" she asked a little weakly as he sat down beside her.

"I'm fine." With a slight smile, he added, "That's a very fetching towel."

"Not something you'll see in Vogue," she acknowledged, "but I didn't think to bring a robe."

"No...you didn't." Their eyes met. "But then, you couldn't have known you'd be staying."

That was true; she would be back in her own bed in her parents' home at that moment had it not been for a too-long day and the feeling that she was imposing on Julian too much to expect him to make a round-trip without any rest.

Or would she? Much as she hated admitting it, even to herself, she realized that there might have been other reasons for her suggesting that they remain at the apartment overnight. Where Julian was concerned, she had always been of two minds, powerfully drawn to him on the one hand, resentful of the power he had over her on the other.

Her small white teeth worried her lower lip as she studied him. He appeared so calm; if it hadn't been for the pulse beating in the hollow between his collarbone she would have thought him completely unaffected by her nearness. That he clearly was affected...filled her with an unbidden sense of pride, even as she recognized where such feelings could lead.

"I think perhaps I should go back to bed," she murmured faintly.

"It might be for the best." His voice was low and husky, caressing her in the faint light. She could feel the warmth of his bare skin and had all she could do not to reach out and touch him.

Her fingers curled under, denying the urge, even as a fresh wave of rain lashed the windows. "Sounds as though the storm is going to last," Julian said.

"Sometimes they do."

"The strongest ones hang in forever."

"It can seem as though they'll never end."

As they spoke, they were moving closer together, drawn by the pull of a force neither could deny. A low sigh escaped Julian when at length the distance between them had narrowed to scant inches.

"Do you have any idea," he asked softly, "how tempting you are?"

She was beyond being able to speak; her only answer was to mutely shake her head. He hesitated a moment, then reached for the crystal snifter in her hand and took it from her. Placing it carefully on the table, he regarded her steadily.

"Arlette, do you understand what's going to happen if we stay like this?"

She took a deep breath and cleared her throat. "Well...it seems fairly obvious to me.... We've always been very attracted to each other."

"What about your notion of being just friends?"

"Yes...there is that.... I suppose you could say it seemed like a good idea at the time." As excuses went, it wasn't much, but it was all she could come up with at the moment.

"Frankly, I never thought it would work." He sounded relieved, as though a great weight had been lifted off his shoulders. His hands were warm on her upper arms, the fingers caressing her gently as he drew her to him.

"We'll be friends, Arlette," he murmured against the silken softness of her throat. "But we'll also be lovers, as we were always meant to be."

Yes, she thought dimly as her hands clasped his shoulders, drawing him down to her. The union of their bodies was a natural outgrowth of everything else they shared. She had been foolish not to recognize that from the beginning. But it was a foolishness born of unhappy memories which she could not quite banish.

"Julian," she breathed softly as he lowered her onto the couch, "don't misunderstand this. It doesn't really change anything."

He was sliding the robe away from her, baring shoulders and arms to his appreciative gaze. "What are you talking about? Of course it does."

"No, I still need to be independent, to run my own life. You have to accept that."

He raised his head enough so that he could stare down at her. His hazel eyes were darker than usual, slashed with golden glints. "Do you really think I'd make the same mistake twice?"

She swallowed thickly. "No, I guess not."

"Count on it. You're a beautiful, passionate woman, Arlette. I want you in my bed. But outside of it, I make no claims on you."

That was what she wanted to hear, so why did it make her feel so empty inside? Unwilling to dwell on that, she twined her arms around his neck and drew his mouth to hers.

"Has anyone ever told you that you talk too much?" she asked.

He laughed, a deep, masculine sound that reverberated up through his chest. "No, but I get the message. Let's find another way to communicate."

She didn't have to ask what that was, not when his warm mouth was delicately tormenting the sensitive lobe of her ear as his hands gently unwound the towel and eased it from her breasts.

For an instant, as she felt herself bared to him, panic flared through her. He steadied her with a slow tender kiss before leaning back to admire what his hands had revealed.

In the dim, storm-tinged light, her breasts were pale and perfectly formed, crowned by rosy nipples that swelled beneath his gaze. Pushing the towel down further, he revealed the narrow span of her waist above the flare of her hips. His hands shook slightly as he dispensed with the covering altogether and let it drop to the floor.

"You are so beautiful," he murmured. "It's a shame to ever cover such loveliness."

Despite the potent headiness of the moment, she laughed softly. "Are you suggesting I should go around naked all the time?"

"No," he corrected swiftly, "only when you're with me."

"Speaking of naked..." Surprised by her own boldness, she found the tie of his pajama bottoms and pulled it loose. Her hands slid beneath the smooth fabric, finding and savoring the hard contours of his hips and buttocks.

"It's been so long," she murmured huskily.

"How long?" he asked, only to instantly amend, "No, don't tell me. I've got no right to ask."

"About other men?" Her fingers tangled in his hair as her body arched against him, the engorged tips of her breasts brushing his chest. "There haven't been any others, Julian. I've only been with a man once, and that was you."

The look he shot her, composed of astonishment mingling with gratitude, touched her to the very core of her being. "I wish I could offer you the same gift," he said raggedly.

The fullness of womanly strength flowed through her as she cradled him closer. "Remember what you said the last time, that it was a good thing one of us knew what he was doing? That still goes."

"Yes, I guess it does." For a moment longer he stared at her, taking in everything from the warm flush of her cheeks and the sparkle of her eyes to the seductive beauty of her body. Then his control broke, and he clasped her to him with a husky groan.

"I'll try to be gentle, Arlette, but I'm not sure I can."

Yet for all the wild force of his passion, he did not hurt her. His caresses were hungry and demanding, but never frightening. It was as though he was determined to draw her fully into the vortex of pleasure with him, so that at the instant of release they would be utterly bound together.

No thought of resistance remained in Arlette's mind. She yielded herself completely to him, instinctively understanding that in such surrender lay the greatest triumph.

When he entered her at last she felt a moment of pinching discomfort, almost as though she was once again a virgin. He felt her flinch and stopped for a few moments, stroking her tenderly and murmuring words of reassurance until her body eased around him, accepting him fully.

Only then did he begin to move within her, at first slowly, then with increasing force. She matched the tempo of his strokes, drawing him further and further into her, until at last the world dissolved around them and there was nothing left except the radiant glow of the joy they had found together.

Afterward, when he had carried her to his bed and she lay in his arms, Arlette listened to the patter of the rain and knew the sweet freedom of no regrets. In retrospect she wondered why she had not understood from the first instant of seeing him again how things had to be.

He was a part of her, as she was of him. It was right and natural that they should be together. At last they could experience the happiness that had been impossible for them years before.

The logistics of their separate lives could be worked out later; for the moment it was enough to know that they were together again.

Waking the next morning, Arlette was at first startled by the solid male body lying against her, but quickly adjusted. Since Julian was still deeply asleep, she was free to study him unobserved.

The hard-boned lines of his face were more relaxed than when he was awake. His sensual mouth was slightly parted, and his chest, bare above the sheet, rose and fell rhythmically.

She reached out a tentative hand, touching him lightly. When he gave no sign of awareness, she grew more daring and let her hand drift downward beneath the sheet.

Although she had now made love with him twice—albeit eight years apart—he was still so new and alien to her as to be vaguely intimidating. But not enough to stop her delicate explorations. At least not until she became suddenly and vividly aware that Julian was most certainly no longer asleep.

"Morning," he drawled, grinning at her fierce blush. When she tried to yank her hand away, his own closed over her wrist, holding her in place. "You were doing just fine. Don't let me interrupt."

"B-but ... I thought you were asleep."

"Honey," he said tenderly as he took in the full extent of her embarrassment, "I'd have to be dead not to respond to you. By the way did you know you're blushing all the way down to your nipples?"

A quick glance at herself confirmed the truth of what he said. She made a grab for the sheet, only to have his other hand push it aside. "Why spoil the view?" he inquired laconically.

"I suppose it's silly to feel shy," she ventured.

"No, not silly, rather ... nice." But if he really thought that, he still wasn't making any allowances for her late-blooming prudery. Instead, he concentrated all his efforts on restoring her to the abandoned woman she had been the night before. And he succeeded more thoroughly than perhaps even he had expected.

When she woke next it was late in the morning and the bed beside her was empty. She showered quickly, and dressed in the same clothes she had worn the day before. Looking at herself in the mirror, she searched for outward signs of what had happened, but instead found only a new glow to her skin and a secret sparkle to her heavy-lidded eyes.

Emerging from the bedroom somewhat tentatively, she heard sounds in the kitchen and followed them. Julian was standing at the counter, grinding coffee beans. He was dressed in jeans and a thin cotton pullover that hugged his chest. Well-worn boots were on his feet, and a leather belt with a silver buckle that she remembered was fastened around his taut waist.

When he heard her come in, he looked up and smiled. "There you are. Ready for coffee?"

She nodded and sat down hastily on a stool, not wanting him to notice how weak the mere sight of him made her feel. He spooned the coffee into a filter, poured boiling water over it and, leaving the brew to drip, popped a couple of English muffins into the toaster.

"I could whip you up some eggs, if you'd like," he offered helpfully.

"I have a feeling I should be doing that," she said.

"Why? It's not your kitchen, and you know I'm perfectly capable of putting together a meal. I've done it often enough."

That was true; living alone as he had, there had been no choice for him except to learn at least the rudiments of cooking or subsist on junk food. As she recalled, he did an excellent stew and was also quite good with hamburgers.

"Doesn't it drive women crazy when you refuse to let them fuss over you? Display their great domestic skills?" she inquired with a smile.

"I suppose there's been a case or two like that, but frankly, I don't care. The women I've dated in the last few years have only served one purpose, which they understood full well."

She flinched at his bluntness. "I see.... No hearts and flowers. Well, perhaps it's just as well to be warned."

He muttered something under his breath, something she was just as glad not to be able to catch, and lifted her bodily out of the chair, holding her firmly when she tried to wiggle away from him.

"Let's get something straight right now," he said. "You never have been and never will be like the other women in my life. If you seriously think that's a possibility, then you are nowhere near as intelligent as I've always believed. What we share is special; I intend to keep it that way."

"Good," she said as firmly as she could manage when her toes were barely brushing the floor. "Then you should understand when I say I don't want to share you with anyone."

He smiled slowly, devastatingly. "Not even my employees, or your family?"

"You know perfectly well what I mean. Not having a lot of strings tied to our relationship isn't the same as not having any responsibilities to each other. I've always been a one-man woman; I don't plan to change now."

"Good," Julian said. "Because I hate to tell you what would happen if you tried."

"Oh yeah? What?"

"Not anything you want to hear," he said ominously.

The corners of Arlette's mouth began to curve upward. "That sounds like a threat—from you and what army?"

"Just me, sweetheart. And I promise you, that's all it will take."

"Big talker."

"Want to go back in the bedroom and discuss it some more?"

"Actually, I'd love to, but I think if we don't get back to Arkady soon, my family really will be worried."

That brought him down to earth, if only reluctantly. "Do you think they might be already?" he asked as he set her down gently and went to see to the coffee.

"They should be," she acknowledged, "but since they know who I'm with, I'm afraid we're in for some very smug looks."

"Still, they may be expecting some sort of announcement...."

"Then they'll just have to be disappointed. They should know better, anyway."

For all her brave talk, she was still a little apprehensive when the sports car turned into the driveway in front of her home and she saw her mother sitting in the porch rocking chair, snapping green beans.

Maria looked up. She frowned slightly as she shaded her eyes from the sun. The chair missed a beat, then resumed rocking. "Afternoon, Arlette, Julian. Looks like another nice day."

"Certainly does," he agreed, his hand on Arlette's elbow as he helped her from the car. "A bit warm, though."

"I made fresh lemonade not an hour ago," Maria said. "Come on in and have some."

"Don't mind if I do."

"How did your interviews go, honey?" her mother asked as she set the beans aside and stood up.

"Just fine," Arlette murmured, hoping her skin didn't look as flushed as it felt. She had imagined being very cool about this, as though she routinely stayed out all night. That wasn't working very well.

"You seem a little warm," Maria observed as they entered the cool shadows of the hallway. "Why don't you go get out of those city clothes while I fix a couple of sandwiches?" In an aside to Julian, she added, "I'll bet you're hungry, aren't you?"

"Starving," he assured her with a grin.

Glad of an excuse to get away, if only briefly, Arlette hurried upstairs. She took off the now wilted suit and blouse, and put them aside to take to the dry cleaner before putting on a well-washed pair of jeans and a cotton shirt. As she was running a brush through her hair she heard the outside door open, followed by the sound of her father's and brother's voices as they greeted Julian.

Holding her breath, she stepped out on the stair landing and unashamedly listened to what was going on downstairs. In the back of her mind was the thought that the men in her family might not be as tolerant as her mother, but that was apparently not the case, at least where Julian was concerned.

When the deep timbre of their laughter floated up the stairs toward her, she didn't know whether to be relieved or exasperated.

Six

Which house is this?" Julian asked, holding up one of the photos spread out on the table. "The Beaufort or the Latour?"

"Latour," Arlette replied, consulting the list. "We've seen it before; I'm sure of that."

"What do you think?"

"I like it, but I still prefer the very first one we saw last week. Remember?"

He nodded and looked at her innocently. "The one with the mirror in the bedroom."

She shook her head wryly and got up to begin clearing the table. They were having supper at the small house he was renting in Arkady until he could settle into something more permanent.

Arlette guessed it had once been a hunting and fishing lodge, since it was situated deep in the bayou. Rough oaken beams criss-crossed the ceiling of the living area, which took up most of the first floor. A large stone fireplace showed signs of heavy use. The kitchen was rudimentary but adequate. A stepladder led to the sleeping loft above them.

"Trust you to think of that," she said as he rose to help her. "Anyway, that's my favorite, not that it matters. It's your decision."

"I value your advice; you know that."

She did, but it was still nice to hear. Standing next to him at the sink as she washed the dishes and he dried, a pleasant feeling of intimacy stole over Arlette. While the hours they spent in the bed upstairs were beyond anything she had ever imagined, she also enjoyed sharing simple, ordinary things with him. He seemed to make every experience, even the most outwardly mundane, somehow special.

"I'm sorry I have to go to Houston tomorrow," she said softly. "But the company I'll be interviewing with is a good one."

"I know," he agreed. "But it's still going to be lonely without you."

That was all he said on the matter, which Arlette appreciated. The old Julian would have argued against her spending any time away from him, especially traveling by herself. He would have worried about her safety, as well as been jealous of other men she might meet. This new Julian apparently was not concerned about either. He took it for granted that she was a grown woman able to look out for herself.

They remained another hour or so at the house before Julian drove her home. Though her family had made no comment about her new relationship with him, she was still unwilling to flaunt it. Especially since she knew their tolerance stemmed in large part

from the expectation that she and Julian would shortly
be making an announcement. As that was not to be
the case, she wanted to avoid making the situation any
more difficult for them than it had to be.

"I'll see you day after tomorow," she said as he
pulled the car up in front of the old clapboard house
and she prepared to get out. Her hand was on the door
latch when she hesitated and turned back. Tentatively, not yet quite sure of herself, she leaned over and
touched her lips to his.

Julian went perfectly still for an instant before
gently enfolding her in his arms and tenderly deepen-
ing the kiss. The touch of his tongue against hers sent
a tremor through Arlette. She pressed closer to him,
heedless of anything except the driving need to dis-
solve the barriers between them. He tasted of mint
toothpaste and the wine they had shared at dinner. The
scent of his sun-warmed skin filled her breath. Her
fingers stroked downward through his thick ebony
hair and across the broad sweep of his shoulders,
warm beneath the thin cotton shirt he wore. She had
the fleeting thought that if she didn't hold on to him
everything in the world might fall away and she would
be left in oblivion.

He moaned deep in his throat and lifted his mouth
from hers, enough to drop feather-light kisses along
the delicate line of her jaw and down her throat. His
teeth raked her earlobe erotically as his hands cradled
her swollen breasts, his thumbs rubbing the nipples
through her blouse.

The hot, sweet wind of desire grew within them
both, threatening to become irresistible, until at last
Julian raised his head and stared down at her reluctantly. His hazel eyes were dark with desire, and his

chest rose and fell raggedly as he muttered, "This isn't the time or the place, unfortunately."

It took Arlette a moment to understand what he was saying, so enraptured was she by his lovemaking. When his words at last reached her, she nodded regretfully. "You're right. I'm sorry; this shouldn't have happened."

"I'm sorry, too," he assured her gravely, though the corners of his mouth twitched. "But then, I've always enjoyed a nice cold shower."

"I haven't," she said, adding with a soft laugh, "but I have a feeling I'd better start."

He left her then, and she went inside, after pausing on the porch step to watch him drive away. Since there was no sign of Louis or his precious truck, she presumed he had gone to visit Debbie. Her parents were in the kitchen, talking quietly. She stuck her head in to tell them she was back.

"Julian didn't come in, dear?" her mother asked.

"No, he has some paperwork to catch up on."

Her father leaned back in his chair. "Has he made up his mind yet about a house?"

"Not yet, but I think he's getting close."

"Which one do you like?"

"The first one we saw, but that doesn't mean anything."

Her parents exchanged a look. "I'm sure Julian will respect your opinion," Maria said.

"Uh...sure...well, if you'll excuse me, I'll be getting to bed."

They nodded and seemed satisfied with what she had told them, but she could feel them waiting until she was safely out of earshot before discussing the matter.

Next morning, over the breakfast table, her father said casually, "I'll be doing some hunting this weekend. Thought maybe Julian would like to come along."

Arlette was buttering a slice of toast. She cut it in half before asking, "Are you going after anything in particular?"

"There's a big old crocodile been coming up in Oncle Pierre's backyard," Louis chimed in before their father could answer. "Seems to have made off with a couple of chickens."

"Might as well go after him, then," Charlie said. "I'll drop by Julian's place and tell him about it." He glanced at his daughter. "'Less of course you'd rather have him to yourself this weekend."

"That's all right," she said hastily, understanding full well what such an admission would mean. Anything that took a Cajun man away from his hunting was considered very serious indeed. "I'll see him when I get back from Houston."

Her father looked faintly disappointed, but said nothing more except to wish her good luck. She felt she was going to need it, since she was strangely lacking in enthusiasm for what should have been a very exciting job prospect. Not until she was on the plane leaving New Orleans did she admit to herself what the problem was: the job in Houston would separate her from Julian, something she was not at all sure she could bear.

As it happened, the job did not turn out to be as interesting as she had thought. While the salary and other benefits were excellent, she would have been spending almost all her time in the lab instead of the field. It was with a clear conscience that she thanked the executive for his time but explained she had something different in mind.

He looked a bit taken aback and suggested they get together to discuss it over dinner. Arlette briefly considered it. During the hour or so they had spent together in his office, the tall, blond man had proven to be intelligent and charming. She didn't doubt that he would be a pleasant dinner companion; nonetheless, she really didn't care to join him.

After politely making her excuses and thanking him once again for his time, she went back downstairs to the lobby, where she found a bank of pay phones, and called the airport. The flight she had originally planned to take back didn't leave for some three hours yet, but if she hurried she would be able to catch an earlier plane.

Returning to New Orleans, she went over the interview in her mind and was reassured that she had acted properly. As important as her job goals were to her, she didn't want them to dominate her entire life. The chances were good that she would be able to find the right position in New Orleans, where she would be free to continue her relationship with Julian.

At the airport she picked up her rental car and drove back to Arkady. Traffic was very light, and she made excellent time, arriving in less than two hours, just as the sun was beginning to set in a red haze beyond the bayous.

Driving by Janine's Place, she noticed Julian's black sports car in the parking lot and, thinking how pleased he would be by her early return, she decided to surprise him.

The surprise, however, was on her. Entering the restaurant, she stood for a moment near the door, scanning the diners. Most of the tables were occupied, and it took her a moment to spot Julian, seated as before in a quiet corner toward the back. Beside him, deep in conversation, was a lovely blonde.

As Arlette watched, her wide blue eyes growing steadily larger, the two laughed companionably, and Julian reached for the blonde's hand.

Shock swept over Arlette, followed hard by pain so severe that for a moment or two she literally could not breathe. Her stomach twisted, and the strength seemed to go out of her legs. She reached quickly for the edge of the bar near the entrance to steady herself.

Fortunately the restaurant was dimly lit and no one had noticed her arrival. She was able to slip out without being observed and make her way to her car, where she slumped in the seat, feeling as though she had run a great distance and was suffering the aftereffects.

Long moments passed before she was able to even think of putting the key in the ignition. Her hands shook so badly that she had to grasp one with the other before she could manage to get the engine started. Barely conscious of what she was doing, she drove away from the restaurant and headed south, out of town.

She had gone perhaps five miles before it occurred to her that driving in such a condition could be very dangerous. She pulled over to the side and leaned back against the seat. With her eyes closed, she struggled to get a grip on herself.

There was undoubtedly a perfectly reasonable explanation for Julian's being with a woman. She might be an old friend who had unexpectedly stopped by, or a business associate.

Except that the odds of someone coming to Arkady by chance were about the same as a blond bombshell being in the oil business.

Arlette took a deep breath and made a valiant effort to be very modern and understanding. Julian was, to all intents and purposes, a free man, just as she was a free woman. He had a perfect right to have dinner with anyone he chose. To be completely fair about it, he had a right to do a lot more than that.

Except he had said he wouldn't.

He had very clearly given her the impression that he expected their relationship to be monogamous. That being the case, who did he think he was to be out wining and dining some other woman while she was away?

The more she thought about it, the angrier Arlette became. Normally she had no difficulty controlling her temper, but this was proving to be an exception. She raged inside at the thought that another woman might know Julian as she did. What was in the past she could live with, but she wasn't about to stand by tolerantly while he added to the notches on his bedpost.

A small voice in the back of her mind warned that she was jumping to unwarranted conclusions, but Arlette ignored it. She gunned the motor and headed back the way she had come.

Passing Janine's Place again, she slowed down enough to confirm that the black sports car was still parked in the lot, then speeded up again. The road to Julian's temporary home was as bumpy and dusty as most in the area. By the time she reached the end of it her arms ached from manipulating the steering wheel, and she was well past the point where she might have reconsidered what she was about to do.

After parking the car out of sight behind the tool shed, she got out and walked rapidly up the steps. As was customary, the door was unlocked. She let herself in and went directly up to the bedroom.

Less than half an hour later she had undressed, showered, dried herself, and gotten between the sheets. If Julian and his lady friend were looking forward to an evening of extracurricular activities, they had better be planning to go to her place. Otherwise they were in for a nasty shock.

Not even such unpleasant thoughts could outweigh the fatigue engendered by the long day that had proven to be so unexpectedly traumatic. Though she valiantly tried to stay awake to reap the full benefit of her presence, her eyes refused to remain open. Almost without her being aware of it, she slipped into sleep.

And awakened to the touch of warm, firm hands drifting over her body.

Arlette turned onto her back languidly, her eyes still closed, only half aware of what was happening to her. She felt as though she was in the midst of a marvelous dream filled with the most exquisite sensations.

Soft ripples of a sultry breeze fluttered over her bare stomach and around her navel. Feather-light caresses teased the insides of her thighs. She moaned faintly and arched toward the source of such enthralling pleasure.

"Easy, sweetheart," a deep voice murmured. "We have all the time in the world."

Hmmm, a talking dream, how nice. She parted her lips and smiled as her slender arms rose. The motion drew her firm breasts higher, making them even more prominent. Her rosy nipples were swollen buds, beckoning the man who loomed above her.

Julian groaned huskily. Coming home to find Arlette nestled in his bed had been a delightful surprise, made all the more so by the discovery that she hadn't bothered with any night clothes. Uncovering her nakedness slowly so as not to wake her, he had been overwhelmed by desire so great that he had to grit his teeth to keep from calling her name.

When she had lain bare before him, pale and slender against the sheets, he had rapidly stripped off his own clothes before joining her on the bed. At the first touch of her body against his, he had been tempted to throw aside all restraint. Only his immense self-control had permitted him to indulge in the gradual seduction of her senses, a seduction that was also awakening her.

His big hands closed around her upper thighs, gently moving them apart. As he did so, he watched her face. Her eyes had fluttered open, at first bemused and uncomprehending, then slowly aware.

"J-Julian..."

"Good evening, sweetheart," he murmured huskily. "May I say you make a delightful dessert?"

"Dessert...?"

"I skipped it at dinner tonight. You'll make up for that just fine."

"D-dinner...the blonde..."

He broke off lightly stroking the undersides of her breasts and lifted his head. "Sheila? How did you know about her?"

She bit her lip, not wanting to answer him, but knowing she had to. "I saw your car at the restaurant, so I went inside."

"Why didn't you come over...?" His eyes darkened as understanding dawned. A wry smile curved his mouth. "You thought I was getting a little action on the side while you were away."

"I'm sorry," she said brokenly. "I had no right."

"The hell you didn't. If I'd been in your place, I would have raised Cain." The leisurely fondling of her breasts resumed, making her ache deep inside. "My lovely Arlette," he went on softly, "I want you to feel possessive about me, to not tolerate the idea of my being with another woman. If you felt otherwise, I'd be hurt."

"You would? But..." She managed to sit up slightly, leaning on her elbows. At first that seemed to be a mistake, since it prompted him to take one of her nipples into his mouth and suck it tenderly. Several moments passed before she could remember what she had meant to say. "Do you mean you weren't with her?"

He broke off his tantalizing love play and shook his head. "Not in the sense that you mean. Sheila Donnelly is a reporter for the *Financial Times*. She's interviewed me in the past. Recently she got word of what I'm up to with Petrex and came down here looking for an exclusive."

"Oh, no, if she prints the story..."

"She won't," he assured her quickly. "At least not until the deal is done. Sheila's too good a reporter not to know when it's better to wait. In return for her patience she'll have the inside track when I'm ready to break the news."

"I see...."

His gaze was gently mocking. "Do you? What I see is an exquisite lady needing to be loved."

Despite the storm of sensations spiralling through her, she managed to smile faintly. "Ladies are for the outside world. In here I prefer being simply a woman.''

"There's nothing simple about it." He lowered his head between her breasts, breathing in the scent of her as he pushed her swollen breasts gently together. The day's growth of his beard scratched lightly against her tender skin.

"Julian."

"Hmmm?"

"Don't do that."

"Why not?" he inquired lazily, not stopping.

"Because it makes me feel . . . too much."

His eyes narrowed slightly, giving him a predatory look. "Then I'll keep on doing it. I want you to feel everything and keep on feeling until you can't stand another moment of it."

The faintly grim undertone to his words roused Arlette slightly from the pool of sensual lethargy into which she was rapidly sinking. She pressed her hands against his shoulders with the vague intention of holding him off.

It didn't work. His strength and determination easily overcame hers as he bore her back onto the bed. Her resistance evaporated swiftly beneath his fiercely demanding caresses.

When they at last joined together, she cried out in relief. Every cell of her being strained toward the completion he offered, yet tantalizingly withheld.

"Julian . . . please . . ."

"Soon," he promised thickly.

"Now." Her nails dug into his back.

"Wildcat," he growled, and drove more deeply into her.

The culmination of their passion was so explosive that for a timeless instant Arlette truly felt that she had been destroyed. Surely it was not possible to recover from so shattering an experience.

Yet she somehow managed to, wrapped safely in Julian's arms, her head on his broad chest and her legs intimately entwined with his. Utterly satisfied and half asleep, she only dimly remembered the anger and hurt that had brought her to his bed. Painful they might have been, but she could not deny that the results had more than made up for her unhappiness.

Only the fact that she had failed to trust him kept her from being utterly content.

They talked about that the next morning after they had shared a shower, with predictable results.

"I don't understand myself," Arlette said as she scrambled eggs at the small stove. She was wearing one of Julian's bathrobes that came down almost to her ankles. The sleeves had to be rolled back several times to free her hands. He glanced appreciatively at the gaping collar, which revealed the delicate swell of her breasts.

"I've never been the jealous type," she went on as she ladled the eggs onto two plates. "But yesterday I really felt as though I could have torn someone's hair out."

"Sheila's, for instance?" he asked with a very male grin.

"No," she said, bringing him his breakfast, "yours."

"Oh. Well, in that case, it's all to the good that I straightened you out, isn't it?"

"Is that what you call it?" she asked, taking the chair next to him at the oak table. "Straightening?"

"It's as good a euphemism as any."

"H-rumph."

"Something caught in your throat?" he inquired solicitously.

"No, I'm fine."

"More coffee?"

She accepted it as graciously as she could manage, and breakfast proceeded without further incident. Once again Julian helped her clear up, prompting her to point out, "You never used to do this."

He rinsed off a plate and placed it in the drainboard before answering. "Do what?"

"Help with the dishes, clean up your own messes, things like that."

"You mean I expected to be waited on."

"No, not exactly. I know you weren't used to that. But I do think you felt that if there was a woman around, she should do it instead of you."

"Did it ever occur to you," he asked quietly, "that I was brought up to feel that way? For that matter, so were you."

"But I decided early on it wasn't for me."

"And I took a while longer to reach that point. So now it doesn't threaten my masculinity to rinse off a dish. Hooray for me."

Despite herself, Arlette laughed. "I hate to tell you this, but you're not what anyone would consider liberated."

He feigned great surprise, unconvincingly. "You're kidding. I thought I had it down pat."

"Uh-uh. You're still clearly convinced that men and women are fundamentally different."

"I had noticed that." His eyes met hers as he asked, "Think there's anything to it?"

"I don't know...might be."

"Maybe we should think about it some more."

"*A lot* more."

He shrugged. "Whatever you say."

She frowned, perversely wishing that he had been more insistent. "You certainly have changed."

"You think so?"

"Don't you?"

He rinsed the last of the dishes and turned off the tap. As he dried his hands, he said, "I read somewhere that a person's character is pretty well formed by the time he's three years old. If that's true, then I haven't changed in quite a while."

"Well...now that you mention it..." She grinned mischievously.

He looked down his nose at her. "I'll have you know I'm considered hot stuff on Wall Street these days, the scourge of companies and all that."

"*Very* impressive."

"Would you by any chance remember the time when you were six years old and I tanned your bottom for going into the bayou alone and getting lost?"

"I seem to recall something about that," she said, judiciously backing away.

"Might I add that you are not too big to have the same thing happen again?"

"Surely you jest. I'm a grown woman, way past any such primitive attempts at control."

"Primitive, was it? Let me tell you something, lady. You haven't encountered primitive yet."

"Oh, really?" Eyeing him with exactly the right mixture of apprehension and enthusiasm, she continued retreating. "If you'll excuse me, I really should get dressed."

"Why? That robe looks a lot better on you than it ever did on me."

"I wouldn't say that," she murmured under her breath."

"What was that?"

"Nothing... I only meant that it doesn't look bad on you."

"Does that mean it looks good?"

"I suppose—" she allowed, "—if a person happens to have a thing for older men."

That did it. Julian crossed the small distance between them in swift, relentless strides. He grasped the lapels of the robe in question and pulled Arlette to him.

She went to her fate with a courage that would have done her forebears proud—and enjoyed every moment of it.

Seven

In the days that followed Arlette found herself on a roller coaster of emotions that was both exhilarating and frightening. On the one hand, being with Julian was everything she could have hoped and more. He brought her to the full realization of her womanhood with consummate skill and tender consideration. In his arms, no doubt or worry touched her.

But away from him things were different. Then she was prey to bouts of apprehension and confusion. An affair was what she had wanted, presumably. So why wasn't she happier about it?

The answer wasn't all that hard to come by. Once before in her life she had experienced a similar sense of dislocation, a feeling of being neither fish nor fowl. It had happened when she was a very young girl on the verge of womanhood, bewildered by the changes going on in her body and concerned about her ability to move gracefully into a future that was as intimidating as it was inevitable.

The present situation was similar in certain respects. When she was with Julian they did all the things that husband and wife would do together. There were even times when she could forget that she wasn't his wife, until something suddenly reminded her. Then that strange sense of dislocation returned.

She was somewhere between single and married, in uncharted territory, where hidden dangers lurked. That much she could figure out; it was what to do about it that eluded her.

"That'll be a dollar forty-nine," Evangeline Cartier said, breaking in on her thoughts. The venerable old woman efficiently stamped the letters she had just weighed for Arlette and placed them in the bag for pickup later that day.

Arlette dug a couple of dollar bills from the pocket of her jeans and handed them over. She was putting her change away when she became aware that Evangeline was watching her carefully.

A slightly wary look entered her blue eyes. Thinking to distract the older woman, she said, "I'm interviewing quite a bit. That's what those letters are about."

"That's fine," Evangeline said, continuing to watch her. Clearly she was not going to be diverted.

Arlette waited resignedly until the older woman nodded, as though having come to some decision in her own mind. Fingering the shawl draped around her stooped shoulders, she said, "Times sure have changed."

"I guess that's so."

"All sorts of things going on nowadays that sure didn't when I was a girl."

Despite herself, Arlette's eyebrows rose. "You expect me to believe that?"

Evangeline shot her a sharp glance. "Didn't I just say it?"

"Yes, but I can't believe that my generation has discovered anything yours didn't know plenty about."

Reluctantly, the older woman chuckled. "Well, now, that is true. But the point is, we had rules about what was right and what was wrong. People were expected to do certain things and not do others."

Arlette sighed and dug her hands into her pockets. She knew what Evangeline was telling her and couldn't disagree with it. "I believe in right and wrong, too. But the world is somewhat more complicated than it used to be. People have more options nowadays."

"Maybe that's not such a good thing."

"When you were a girl," Arlette asked, "did you ever think about leaving here, going out into the world?"

"Yes...sometimes...but I was married at fifteen and had a baby a year till I was twenty-three, so there wasn't much chance of going anywhere."

"That's my point. Today you would have the chance. But to take it, you'd have to give up other things."

"Such as?"

"Security...simple answers...a smooth niche to slip into without any snags. You have to make choices for yourself now, and take risks."

Evangeline thought about that, her deeply lined face calm in reflection. Quietly she said, "Seems to me a person could get hurt doing that."

"Yes," Arlette agreed slowly, "that can happen."

They were both silent for a moment then Evangeline smiled reassuringly. "Julian's a good man. I know some people around here used to look down on him, but I was never one of them. He always seemed to me to have a kind of substance others were missing."

Arlette swallowed against the sudden tightness in her throat. She didn't want to think about Julian as he had once been. Nothing could be more inappropriate than to pity him, considering what he had become. But even so, a wave of tenderness washed over her as she thought of him.

"I'd better be going," she said.

Evangeline nodded placidly. "Sure, honey. Take care of yourself now."

She was halfway out the door when the older woman called, "Oh, by the by, you are coming to the wedding, aren't you?"

"Wedding?"

"Jeannie Devereux's marrying Paul Rondale day after tomorrow. The whole town's invited."

She had heard her parents saying something about that at the breakfast table. "Oh, sure, thanks for reminding me. I'll look forward to it."

Evangeline was still smiling as Arlette hurried out the door.

She walked back slowly to her car, deep in thought. Jeannie Devereux was a pretty, dark-haired girl who lived about a mile from Arlette's parents' home. She was five years younger than Arlette, so they had never been close, but she remembered that Jeannie had wanted to be a teacher. What had happened to that ambition?

Perhaps nothing. Teaching was one of the few jobs that could be combined relatively easily with raising a family; that was why so many women had traditionally chosen it. Wryly she acknowledged to herself that exploring for oil was a different matter entirely.

While at the post office she had picked up the day's mail. There were several envelopes for her, including one from a company she had interviewed with in New Orleans. She opened it swiftly and scanned the single typewritten page.

It took a moment for the words to sink in. When they did, she exhaled softly and reread the letter more slowly. They were extremely impressed with her qualifications and wished to offer her a position on their exploration team. If she found the terms acceptable, she was invited to call the office to arrange a starting date.

Fairly hugging herself with delight, she hurried home to tell her parents the good news.

They took it calmly, but with obvious pride. "Well, now," her mother said as she broke off kneading dough and hugged her daughter. "I never had a moment's doubt. Congratulations, honey."

"The same goes for me," her father assured her as he beamed a smile. He was in the house for lunch, but would shortly be returning to work. Not, however, before letting his daughter know how proud he was of her. "You're the first one in our family to do anything like this. You'll have to excuse me if I do a little bragging."

"A little?" her mother repeated with a laugh. "Like as not you'll be hollering it from the rooftops."

"Hollering what?" Louis asked as he came into the kitchen and headed over to the sink to wash his hands.

"Arlette got that job she wanted," his father told him. "In New Orleans."

"Hey, that's terrific, Sis. When do you start?"

"I don't know yet, exactly," she said. "But I imagine it will be soon. When I talked with them, they told me they were anxious to get someone in quickly."

"Then you'll be leaving here..." her mother said softly.

"But I won't be going far," Arlette swiftly pointed out. "Not like last time. I can come home on weekends, and you can come and visit me."

"I'd like that," Louis declared. "New Orleans is one hell of a town."

"If you do go see your sister there," his father said, "you'll behave yourself." Turning to Arlette, he added, "I don't know honey, I'm a little worried about your living there alone."

"But I did it in New York."

"And we lost some sleep over that. You can't really blame us for wanting you to be safe."

"No, of course not...." What could she say to them? New Orleans was no worse than many other cities, and better than some. She certainly wasn't about to take any foolish chances, but the fact was that they did have a point; living alone could be dangerous.

"Look," she said after a moment, "let's discuss this some other time. I'll have to go to New Orleans to look for a place to live; maybe I can come up with something that will allay your concerns."

Her parents exchanged a glance, but said nothing further. Yet she couldn't shake the thought that something had occurred to them both which they were not letting her in on.

Not that it mattered. She had enough to concern herself with after she placed a call to the company in New Orleans, accepted their offer and made arrangements to start on the first of the new month. That gave her about ten days to get her affairs in order.

Lord, what a misnomer that was, she thought grimly. There was only one affair she had to worry about and that, to all outward appearance was going swimmingly. Certainly Julian seemed perfectly content. When they had dinner together that night he insisted on opening a bottle of champagne to celebrate her new position.

"To everything you want, Arlette," he said as he raised his glass to her. "I hope it will prove as worthwhile as you believe."

She took a sip and smiled faintly. "I'm not sure quite how to take that. It sounds vaguely ominous."

"Not at all. I'm merely expressing my wish that you never know disappointment."

"You're too late," she said quietly. "I've already known it."

He looked at her over the rim of his glass. "When?"

"When I discovered it's impossible to have everything, of course. Did you really think I hadn't figured that out yet?"

"Sometimes," he said slowly, "I don't know what to think about you."

She brushed a strand of hair away from her cheek impatiently and went on determinedly. "Life's less pleasant realities are not exactly a secret to me, Julian. I discovered them when I was eighteen and you presented me with an ultimatum."

"It always comes back to that, doesn't it?"

He sounded so unhappy that she relented, slightly. "I'm not blaming you, honestly. But please don't make me out to still be a naive little girl. I'm not that at all."

"Not naive," he acknowledged, "but perhaps a bit more optimistic than is good for you."

"What do you mean?" she asked, genuinely puzzled.

He looked away, his hazel eyes fathomless. "Nothing. Forget it."

"Don't brush me aside like that. I want to know what's going on in your mind."

"Why should I tell you?" he demanded suddenly. "What gives you the right to know my thoughts?"

Shocked, she said the first thing that occurred to her. "Why? Because I love you, of course."

He laughed harshly, making her wince. "Love? Is that what you call it? We do very well in bed together, but that's hardly love."

"It's not . . . ?"

"Not by itself," he went on implacably. "There's a great deal more to it."

"You sound like an expert," she said angrily.

"Hardly, but I do know enough about it not to try to fool myself. We aren't in love with each other."

"Thanks for telling me." She got up abruptly, put her glass down on the table so firmly that some of the golden liquid splashed out, and walked quickly away.

Julian was after her in a flash. His hand closed around her arm, dragging her back to him. "You walked out on me once," he rasped. "I'm not about to let you do it again."

"Let me? Where do you come off telling me what I can and cannot do? If I want to leave, I will." She was beyond anger now, barely able to see him because of the hurt tears blurring her vision. Not in love? What did he know about it anyway?

"No," he insisted, refusing to let her go. Instead he pulled her closer, until she could not help but be vividly aware of the warm hardness of his body against her own. "Why are you so upset?" he demanded softly, his breath teasing her cheek. "Is love that important to you?"

"No...yes. I don't know," she finally admitted with a broken sob. Hating for him to see the full extent of her anguish, she doubled her fists and pushed them fiercely against his chest in a futile effort to break his hold on her.

"You'll only hurt yourself if you keep on with that," he said mildly.

At that instant Arlette truly believed she hated him. How could he be so callous, so completely unconcerned about her feelings? Didn't she mean anything to him at all?

"Let me go," she demanded. "I don't want to be near you."

"You liked it fine up till now," he reminded her cruelly. "Before dinner, for instance."

"Why you . . . Don't you have any sensitivity at all? Let me go!"

In her frantic efforts to get away from him she lashed out unthinkingly, striking him in the calf with the sharp heel of her shoe. Julian grunted in pain, but his grip did not slacken.

"Why are you so upset?" he demanded harshly. "Because I forced you to face the truth?"

"Your truth, not mine. Keep it; I don't want anything to do with it, or you!"

"Liar," he said, pushing her back until she was trapped between the wall and his hard body. Even as he pressed against her, making her vividly aware that their struggles had aroused him, she was dimly conscious of his hands behind her back, protecting her from contact with the sharp molding.

"You love what I make you feel," he grated. "If there is love between us, that's where it lies. Admit it."

"No, it isn't true," she protested heatedly, turning her head from side to side to try to prevent him from kissing her. "I was stupid enough to fall in love with you, more fool me. But that doesn't mean I have to go on being so dumb. I got over you once, and I can do it again."

"*You* got over *me*," he said incredulously. "Don't tell me you're suggesting you cared for me before?"

"Of course I did!" she cried. "I wanted to share my life with you, but you insisted that everything be on your terms. You wanted to own me; I couldn't stand that."

The burnished darkness of his lean face warned her that she had touched a nerve. When his hand tangled in her hair, pulling her head back, she cried out, almost in fear.

Instantly he relented, though only slightly. Still forcing her to look at him, he rasped, "Yes, it's true, I would like to own you. Every beautiful silken inch. I'd like to have you at my beck and call every moment. I'd like to be able to possess you whenever I wish, and however."

A shiver ran through Arlette as her breath caught in her chest. Unable to speak, she stared at him as though mesmerized. The erotic images his words conjured up made her feel unbearably weak. All too easily she could see herself as his helpless slave, utterly subject to his will.

Except that she could never allow herself to fall into such a degraded position. Not so long as an ounce of pride and strength remained.

"I can't force you to let me go," she said stonily, "but I can tell you that if you do what I think you're considering, I'll never forgive you."

"And what's that?" he demanded huskily, staring down at her. "Do you imagine I have rape in mind?"

"You certainly have it somewhere," she muttered, trying to move her lower body away from his, where the thrusting proof of his masculinity reminded her all too forcibly of the joys they had shared. This was not the time to be thinking of that, not when she had to concentrate on how much his denial of love had hurt her.

He laughed and wrapped his arm more firmly around her, holding her immobile. Ignoring her outraged exclamation, he took her mouth in a deep, evocative kiss that for a moment at least banished all thought of anything except the passion flaring between them.

When he at last raised his head, he said huskily, "You can respond like that to me and still suggest I'd have to rape you?"

"I won't let you take advantage of me like this," she insisted stubbornly, hoping he wouldn't notice the throbbing drumbeat of her pulse, or the rapid rise and fall of her breasts as she struggled to breathe. "You've as good as said that you don't care anything for me."

He hesitated a moment, his eyes more gold now than hazel, like rays of sunlight bursting through storm clouds. "I care," he said thickly. "Too much.

I'd like nothing better than to be able to take you and not feel anything but sheer physical release."

"As though I were a whore," she gasped, "or worse, an object."

"But you're not either," he murmured, his lips nuzzling her throat, finding the delicate pulse points unerringly. "You're Arlette, special, unique, the woman I've never been able to forget."

A sob broke from her, caught instantly in his mouth as he devoured her lips hungrily. Anger, pain, resistance, all dissolved beneath the onslaught of need he unleashed in her. Her hands splayed across his broad back, pressing against the rock-hard muscles, as she strove to be closer to him than the barriers of their clothes allowed.

She was hardly aware when he abruptly broke off the kiss and, with a deep, guttural sound, lifted her into his arms. The stepladder to the sleeping loft was only a few yards away, but Julian apparently thought that was too far. He laid her instead on the thick rug beneath the skylight, through which the stars glowed brightly.

His fingers trembled slightly on the buttons of her blouse, but he made short work of them before also unfastening her skirt and stripping it off. Lying before him in nothing but her lacy bra and thin scrap of her panties, with her chestnut hair tumbling in a silky cloud around her head, she felt almost unbearably vulnerable. For an instant a measure of the fear she had experienced earlier returned. But it vanished as she recognized the hesitation in Julian and knew that he was unable to hurt her.

Raising her slender arms, she reached out to him. With a faint smile she said, "We can fight any old time. Right now, let's do something better."

"Witch," he rasped as he yanked off his shirt and tossed it aside. It was followed swiftly by his boots and jeans, leaving him in nothing but the briefs that did little to hide the urgency of his need.

"You drive me insane," he said as he lowered himself to her, letting her feel for an instant the full measure of his weight and strength. "I can't get enough of you. Every time I think I'm finally satisfied, the hunger starts all over again, only worse."

"Don't you know it's the same for me?" she murmured, stroking the bare expanse of his back. "When I'm apart from you, you're constantly in my thoughts. And when we're together..."

"Yes?" he drawled, his customary male confidence undiminished by his need for her. "What's it like then, sweetheart? Tell me."

"I won't," she protested, laughing. "You've got enough of a swelled head as it is."

"Well, something's certainly swollen."

Despite herself she flushed, prompting him to chuckle indulgently. "After all these years you still react almost like a virgin." His smile faded as he said more gently, "But then, you practically are. You're so instinctively skillful that I keep forgetting how new this really is to you."

"Wouldn't you say I'm learning fast?" she gasped as he undid the front clasp of her bra and spread the two sides apart. Her nipples were so erect that they ached, and she longed for the soothing ministration of his tongue.

"You always were a good student," he murmured huskily as he lowered his head, his lips at first just brushing her in delicate caresses that did nothing to satisfy her need.

"Julian, please . . . give me more. . . ."

Her hands tangled in his hair, trying to press him closer, but he caught her wrists and drew her arms over her head, holding them as he stared down at her.

The silken tumult of her hair drew his gaze, as did the sapphire glow of her eyes and the warm flush of her cheeks. Her lips, moist and slightly swollen from his kisses, were parted a little. He could see the white gleam of her small teeth through them.

He lowered his gaze further, taking in the ripe beauty of her breasts rising and falling agitatedly. Against his burnished skin her own looked like cream lightly touched by honey. He longed to taste every part of her, but not so long as any doubt of her wishes remained in his mind.

"Are you really willing, Arlette?"

How could he ask such a question? Every cell in her body must be telling him how much she wanted him.

She was about to say as much when he went on relentlessly. "I don't want there to be any doubt in your mind. You were afraid before; I saw that. Do you still think I would force you?"

"No," she gasped as his big hand cupped her breast, the callused thumb rubbing over her nipple. "I don't think that anymore." Because he wouldn't have to. She was powerless to deny him anything.

"Good," he groaned huskily. Yet though he appeared convinced, he did not release her hands. Still holding them, he pushed a finger beneath the elastic of her panties and pulled them down. For a moment he raised himself off her, removing his own last garment. Then there was nothing more to separate them as their bodies cleaved together with explosive force.

Arlette cried out helplessly. The sheer power of his masculinity stunned her. She was free at last to touch him, and she took full advantage of that. The quickening rhythm of his body told her how much he was affected by her caresses.

Emboldened, she arched upward, taking him deeper into herself. He moaned her name against her heated skin and grasped her tightly to him. Later she would find bruises in the soft flesh of her hips where he had held her so fiercely in his passion, but just then she was aware of nothing except the shattering fulfillment that overtook them both at the same time, reaching far beyond the boundaries of their bodies and making their spirits fully one.

If only temporarily. Returning slowly to full consciousness in the safety of Julian's arms, Arlette was swept by an unexpected sense of melancholy.

She longed to tell him again that she loved him, but was afraid to do so, lest she provoke the same denial. Could he be right? Was it possible that what they had just shared was not love?

Reluctantly she admitted that he was far more experienced than she was, and therefore much more likely to understand the true nature of the emotions flowing between them. But he was also a man who had learned at an early age to expect little from life other than what he could wrest on his own terms. To him, the thought that love might be given generously and without strings attached might seem so unlikely as to be impossible.

In the moments before exhaustion overtook her, she thought that it was almost as though he was challenging her to prove the truth of her feelings. Not consciously, perhaps, but that could easily turn out to be the effect of his angry denial.

Yet how could love be proven? Through self-sacrifice? The very idea was a contradiction. If she sacrificed herself, then she would no longer exist to love him. He would possess only the shell of a woman instead of the complete person she was now.

Could she ever make him see that should not be?

So far they had been lucky. Making love again as they had, there was a chance for them to make a new beginning. How many people were ever that fortunate?

She couldn't bear the thought that they might throw such an opportunity away because of misunderstandings, yet the possibility did exist.

Soon she would be starting her job, and then Julian would have to come to terms with the full impact of who and what she was: no longer the sweet young girl so smitten with him, or the frightened young woman defiantly rejecting his authority.

In the fullness of time, and not without difficulty, she had come into her own. She liked the person she was now, and did not want to lose any part of herself. Yet she also wanted Julian.

Was it possible to have both?

Eight

We ought to be back for supper, honey," Charlie said as he kissed his wife goodbye. "But if we get held up, don't wait for us."

"All right," Maria agreed reluctantly. "You all be careful now."

Louis and Julian promised that they would, as did Charlie, then all three tromped out to the Jeep, where they had earlier loaded the equipment needed for the crocodile hunt.

Arlette went after them, standing on the porch with her arms wrapped around herself, even though the predawn air was not particularly chilly.

Mist rose off the bayou, cloaking it in ghostly raiment. Far off in the distance an owl hooted sleepily, done with its night's hunting and eager for rest.

She shivered, her eyes going to the tall, ebony-haired man getting into the Jeep. He turned slightly, saw her, and lifted a hand. She returned the wave and tried to smile, without much success. The strange melancholy that had settled over her the night before still lingered. She could not shake it, try though she did.

"Come inside, honey," Maria said, touching her arm lightly. "I saved some coffee when I filled the Thermos for the men. Care for a cup?"

"Sounds good." She followed her mother inside and back to the kitchen, which even at such an early hour was filled with the good smells of fresh-baked cinnamon rolls, bacon, and strong chicory coffee.

As Maria filled two cups and set several rolls on a plate, she said, "Oncle Pierre will certainly be glad to get rid of that croc. I hear it killed a small pig yesterday."

"That's terrible," Arlette said, not really surprised, since she had known all her life how dangerous the crocodiles that lived in the bayous could be. Often more than ten feet in length and weighing hundreds of pounds, they were as dangerous to hunt as a wild bear or lion.

"Dad's done this before, hasn't he?" she asked as she joined her mother at the scrubbed oak table.

Maria nodded. "He has, but not in quite a few years. I think you had just turned eight when he shot the croc that had killed Evangeline's little dog."

"I remember that. It had threatened several children, too."

"That's right. For several weeks we were afraid to let any of you play near the bayous. All the mothers kept their kids inside rather than take the risk."

"Every man around here was looking for that croc," Arlette said reminiscently, "but it was Dad who found it."

"Not on purpose," Maria said with a smile. "Oh, he'd been looking all right, but when he didn't have any luck, he decided to do some crawfishing. Wouldn't you know that awful big thing had the same idea?"

Arlette grimaced, thinking of what it must have been like to come on the huge primordial lizard in the gloom of the bayous without warning. "At least this time he's not alone," she said, as much to comfort herself as her mother.

"That's certainly better. Your father is still a good shot, and Louis can take the lid off a can of beans at fifty paces. But nobody outshoots Julian."

"Is that why Dad asked him along, because he's a sharpshooter?"

"Partly," her mother said, "but he also just likes his company. You know he's thought of Julian as a son for years now."

There was no criticism in Maria's voice, yet Arlette couldn't help but stiffen slightly. She found herself thinking about how Julian seemed both willing to accept her parents' love for him and to return it. Why couldn't he do the same for her?

Of course, her parents had never disappointed or rejected him. She had done both.

"Honey," her mother broke in softly, "is something wrong?"

"What? Oh, I'm sorry, I was just thinking."

"Not about anything pleasant, from the look of it." Maria hesitated a moment before adding, "You know I don't want to interfere. That's the quickest way to drive a wedge between a grown child and a parent. But if you need to talk to someone, perhaps another woman, I hope you'll remember that I'm here."

Arlette blinked hard against a sudden sheen of tears. When her vision cleared she smiled. "Thanks, Mom, I appreciate that. If I could put what's bothering me in words, I'd certainly tell you."

"It is hard sometimes to express our deepest feelings," Maria agreed sympathetically. "Why, I remember when I first met your father, I was afraid to even let him know I liked him."

Startled, Arlette asked, "Why? I thought the two of you were crazy about each other right from the start."

"Sure we were, but neither one of us found that out until later. I guess we were afraid of getting hurt."

"When you finally told him," Arlette asked slowly, "how did he take it?"

"Oh, he didn't believe me. He thought I was too young to know my own mind." Maria chuckled fondly. "I had a dickens of a time convincing him."

"How did you manage it?"

Her mother shot her a very womanly look. "How do you think?"

"Oh...that way. Well, it worked, didn't it?"

"Thank heaven, although I wasn't so sure of that back then."

Arlette frowned and put down her coffee cup. "What do you mean?"

"My family got wind of what was going on, and my father and brothers went to have a little chat with Charlie. Back then that kind of thing happened. The upshot of it all was that we got married a little bit sooner than we might have."

"You mean you had a shotgun wedding?" Arlette asked in astonishment. This was something she had never even heard hinted at before.

"Not exactly," Maria allowed. "Father Montclair would never have let any guns in the church. Let's just say that Charlie was getting some very threatening looks until the vows were said and the certificate signed."

"Good lord, I can't imagine Dad in a situation like that. What he must have thought . . ."

"He thought he'd been trapped," Maria said succinctly, "and as a result the first few months of our married life were a bit . . . turbulent."

"How did you cope? It couldn't have been easy."

"It wasn't. In fact, it got so bad that I finally told your father I thought it would be a good idea for us to go our separate ways. Even though it would have caused quite a scandal back then, I just couldn't see us being miserable for the rest of our lives."

"He didn't take you up on it?" Surely not, since they were still together.

Maria stirred her coffee reflectively. "When I suggested it, he seemed quite startled, but he said fine, if that was what I wanted, he wouldn't stand in my way. I don't mind telling you, I was crushed. You see, I'd been having all sorts of romantic daydreams about him realizing how much he loved me and the two of us living happily ever after." She smiled gently. "For a while, it seemed as though my dreams were doomed to the sorest disappointment."

"You didn't actually separate . . . ?"

"No, I got as far as throwing my clothes into a battered old suitcase. Charlie came in when I was about halfway done, looked at the mess I was making and said, all things considered, maybe it would be just as well if he didn't inflict me on my family again."

"That was certainly romantic," Arlette said wryly. "What did you do?"

"Told him what he could do with his arrogant opinions and his stuffed-shirt attitudes. As I recall, he then informed me that I was spoiled rotten, an unprincipled schemer and the most infuriating woman he'd ever encountered."

"Uh-oh, sounds as though things were heating up."

"Indeed. Without going into too much detail, I will admit that you were born exactly nine months later to the day."

Arlette sat back, thinking about what her mother had told her. She didn't have to wonder why Maria had chosen that moment to reveal so personal a story. It was undoubtedly meant to illustrate the need for honest communication within relationships. If she and Arlette's father had been more open with each other from the beginning, they could have avoided considerable misunderstandings. Instead, pride and fear of their own vulnerability had kept them at odds until it was almost too late.

Were she and Julian the same? She didn't think so, at least not exactly, but she might be wrong. "Julian and I talk," she said softly. "I'm just not sure what we're saying is true."

"Don't you know, at least for yourself?"

"I should," Arlette acknowledged. "Certainly I'm not trying to mislead him, or myself. But I have a feeling the situation is more complicated than I want to admit."

"Because you're trying to have both a career and Julian?" When she nodded, her mother said gently, "I'm sorry that's not something I can advise you about, since it's completely outside my experience."

"You didn't think of being a homemaker as a career?"

Maria laughed gently. "We never even used that word—homemaker. It's of more recent vintage. For women of my generation it was simply a matter of being a wife and mother; one was part of the other."

"I can almost envy you," Arlette murmured, "except that I know it could never have been easy to do all you did."

"There were times when I wasn't sure if I was coming or going," Maria agreed matter-of-factly. "But it was all worth it in the end."

"I wonder if I'll be able to say that," Arlette mused. "Years from now, will the price I've paid seem fair?"

"No one can promise you that for sure, but it does seem to me that no amount of achievement in any area is really worthwhile unless it can be shared." Having said that, Maria stood up, patted her daughter gently on the arm, and went to start her bread dough rising.

The day seemed to pass very slowly. Arlette ran some errands, wrote several letters to friends in New York, ironed a pile of her clothes, and helped her mother around the house. She found it difficult to concentrate, since at the faintest sound from the road she was at the window looking out, hoping to see the Jeep returning.

Even so, she wasn't really expecting it until after supper. When it appeared suddenly, well before then, surprise darted through her. She came down the outside stairs from the second floor to find her mother already out on the porch. Together they watched the vehicle approach up the dusty road.

"Something's wrong," Arlette breathed, hardly aware that she did so. In the next instant she was running down the steps across the front yard, reaching the Jeep even before it stopped.

Julian was slumped in the back seat, held partially upright by a grim-faced Louis, who was trying without much success to steady him during the bumpy ride. As Arlette ran up her brother said, "Take it easy, Sis. If you think he looks bad, you ought to see the croc."

Though she knew he was only trying to reassure her, she gritted her teath angrily. Julian's face was ashen, blood splattered his shirt, and his left arm was hanging limply at his side. A sob rose in her throat, only to be bitten back as her mother said firmly, "Go in the house and start water boiling. We'll need sutures and bandages; you know where they're kept. Lift him real careful now," she instructed her husband and son as together they began to ease Julian from the Jeep.

Arlette allowed herself a single backward glance before racing into the house. She banged open cabinet doors until she found the large stainless steel pot she was looking for, then burned her fingers getting the stove lit. That done, she hurried to the pantry, where she found the medical kit her mother always kept well stocked. Since Arkady had no doctor of its own and the nearest hospital was some thirty miles away, everyone who lived there learned to be very self-reliant. Cuts, abrasions, even simple fractures, were routinely tended at home.

Arlette had the kit opened and supplies laid out on a clean cloth on the kitchen table when Louis and her father came through the door, supporting Julian betwen them. He was conscious but seemed unsure of where he was, until his eyes lit on her.

"Arlette..."

"Sit down," she ordered abruptly, struggling to hide her terror. He was lowered into the nearest chair, where he remained unresistingly as they began to cut away his blood-stained shirt.

"It's all right," he murmured softly. "I'm not badly hurt."

"Of course not," she snapped. "You'll rest for a minute or two and be ready to run a marathon. God forbid anyone should think you're not Superman."

Her voice broke and she bit her lip, fiercely blinking back the tears she absolutely would not let fall. Removing his shirt had revealed a vicious gash across his upper arm as far as his shoulder. She didn't have to ask what had caused it; only the razor-sharp teeth of a crocodile could inflict such damage. "He could have taken your arm off."

Julian shrugged, winced at the pain the movement caused, and stayed still.

"I never saw anything like it in all my born days," Charlie was saying. "That monster has to be fifteen feet long, easy. And as vicious as they come."

"He got away?" Maria asked softly as she began to bathe the wound. Her touch was as gentle as possible, but Arlette knew it must be painful. Even so, Julian bore it stoically.

"Got away?" her father repeated. "Not by a long shot. Julian got him point blank between the eyes *after* his arm got messed up. Finest shooting I've ever seen."

"I'll say," Louis agreed. "For a minute there I thought we were goners. That thing was trying to tip over the boat. Came pretty close to succeeding, too. That's how Dad ended up in the water."

"You fell in?" Maria asked with a barely suppressed gasp. Under such circumstances a boat was the only safety men had. Falling into the water where a vicious croc hunted meant a grisly death.

"Julian hauled him out," Charlie explained quickly. "He'd just gotten me over the side of the boat when that critter struck. Tried to take his arm right off. Could hardly believe my eyes. There's that monster snapping away and Julian just reaches for his gun, gets hold of it one handed and fires. Croc took off like a bat out of hell, but he didn't look mortally wounded. You know they're about the toughest things on earth to kill. He got maybe thirty feet swimming underwater before Julian took a bead on him." Charlie shook his head in awe. "There he was, blood gushing out of his arm, standing up in the boat calm as you please, waiting till he got a clean shot. When he did, that was the end of the croc."

Arlette swayed slightly, her hands tightening on the back of the chair. She could picture the scene all too vividly: the mist-shrouded bayous filled with hidden dangers; the deadly primordial beast; the men locked in mortal struggle with it.

"The bleeding is stopped," Maria said softly, "but you'll need half a dozen stitches or so. We can go over to the hospital if you want or I can do it. Take your pick."

Julian raised his eyebrows sardonically. He appeared to have fully recovered from the shock of what had happened; his color was already returning despite what must certainly have been a heavy loss of blood, and his hazel eyes were clear. "Would I take a doctor over the finest embroiderer in Louisiana?" he asked teasingly.

Maria laughed. "I guess if you have to have a scar, it might as well be a pretty one."

Arlette shook her head weakly. How could they all joke about such a terrible thing? Didn't they realize that Julian had almost been killed?

"Honey, did you put the needles to boil?" her mother asked.

When Arlette didn't answer at once, Julian reached back and put his hand on hers. Quietly he said, "Don't let me down now, sweetheart. It's almost over."

His gentle words gave her courage. She took a deep breath and went to get what her mother would need. Half an hour later the suturing was mercifully done, a bandage was in place, and Julian was relaxing with her father and brother over a steaming plate of gumbo.

"Tomorrow," Charlie said, "we've got to go back to the bayou and haul that croc out. I want to see him again for myself, and I want everybody else to get a look at him."

"What'll you do with the skin?" Louis asked Julian. "Ought to bring a fancy price."

"Maybe, if I knew anything about butchering croc, which I don't. Why don't you take care of it for me?"

Louis hesitated a moment, obviously tempted but not wanting to seem too eager. "If I did, I'd expect to split the profits with you."

"Whatever. Just do me a favor and don't save me any of the meat."

Everyone laughed at that, even Arlette. She'd had crocodile once and hadn't thought much of it, though there were those who claimed it tasted like chicken.

When she mentioned this, her mother nodded and said, "Speaking of chickens, you know little Jeannie Devereux's getting married."

Arlette nodded. The reference to chickens did not faze her, though it would undoubtedly have puzzled any non-Cajun. "Are you taking a hen?" she asked her mother.

"Of course. So are all the other married women. Jeannie's made it clear she wants a real old-fashioned wedding."

"Oh, lord," Charlie groaned, "that means none of us will be able to pick up our heads for a couple of days afterward."

"Speak for yourself," Maria informed him. "At least the women will behave themselves."

Her father laughed good-naturedly and they went on to talk of other old-fashioned customs that were regaining popularity.

"You should have been here last Mardi Gras," Louis said, "when we had the *gumbo gros*. Mom got so mad when we tried to take more than one of her chickens for it."

"One is all the men are allowed to take from each woman," Maria said firmly. "The chickens have always been our way of earning pocket money. You should be glad we even let you have that much."

"Oncle Pierre fell off his horse while we were out collecting for the gumbo pot," Louis went on, grinning. "But I'm not sure he noticed."

"As the Tex-i-ans say," Charlie added, giving the name its slightly derisive Cajun pronunciation, "a good time was had by all."

"I'm sorry I missed it," Julian said. "Maybe next year."

"Yes," Charlie said thoughtfully, glancing from him to Arlette and back again. "Maybe so. How's the arm feeling?"

"Fine. Ought to be back to normal in a couple of days."

Maria scoffed at that. "More like a couple of weeks, and don't try to tell me it isn't hurting, because I know better. It would be a good idea for you to stay the night, Julian, just in case a fever sets in."

"I'm sure it won't, but—"

"I'd really feel a lot better if you'd stay," she went on. "After all, you got hurt protecting Charlie, so it's our responsibility."

Julian tried to convince her otherwise, but she remained unbending. At length he gave in graciously and agreed to spend the night, though he insisted she'd be sorry when she saw how much he'd want for breakfast.

"I'll make up a bed in the guest room," Arlette said quietly when supper was over. She had listened to the conversation without taking much part in it. Her mind remained on the injury Julian had suffered, and how terrified she had felt when she saw him barely conscious and bleeding.

Somehow being afraid for him was far worse than any fear she had ever felt for herself. Where he was concerned, she was helpless to control her emotions. Despite all her claims to independence, her life was becoming intimately intertwined with his. She needed him to a degree she had never experienced before, not even when she had been so much younger and more vulnerable.

Paradoxically, it seemed that the more control she had over her own life, the more she longed for him to fully share it with him.

She was still thinking about that an hour or so later when they said good night. After the long, tension-filled night, everyone felt the need to get to bed early, except for Louis, who went off to visit his Deborah and undoubtedly regale her with the croc story. Maria and Charlie withdrew to their bedroom, the lamps were turned off and the house settled down for the night.

Arlette lay awake in her small bed, staring out at the silver glow of the moon visible through the thin curtains covering her windows. It was warmer than usual, and she had kicked the sheet off; the thin cotton nightgown she wore provided more than ample covering.

Tired though she was, she could not sleep. The knowledge that Julian was only a few yards away in the guest room kept her wakeful. She didn't believe any more than Maria had that he wasn't hurting. Having seen the wound for herself, she was certain it must be extremely painful. He'd had a couple of beers at supper, but they would hardly be enough to put a dent in his discomfort. She wondered how he would be able to get the rest he so badly needed if he was to recover.

A sound from the next room made her sit suddenly upright against the pillows. Julian was moving around. She heard a window open and listened for the sound of footsteps that would tell her that he was returning to bed. When she didn't hear them, she slid her feet onto the floor and stood up.

For a moment she hesitated, then opened her door and slipped into the hallway. His door was closed. She knocked very lightly, and when she heard his muffled "Come in," eased it open.

He was standing with his back to the window, wearing the pajama bottoms her father had loaned him. They were a little small, and snugly outlined the taut narrowness of his hips and the corded muscles of his thighs. Moonlight flowed behind him, outlining the shape of his wide shoulders and chest, and emphasizing the proud tilt of his head.

"Are you all right?" Arlette whispered. She had shut the door behind her, but even so she was concerned about disturbing her parents, asleep not very far away.

"I'm fine," he insisted curtly, then added more gently, "You shouldn't be here."

"I know... it's awkward... but I'm worried about you."

He smiled faintly. "Believe it or not, I'm not incapable of taking care of myself."

She refused to be put off by his mocking tone. "I know that, but you had a bad accident. If you need something for the pain..."

"Are you offering to kiss it and make it better?"

"Fine, joke around all you want, but don't think for a minute that you're fooling me. That damn croc nearly took your arm off. You should be in a hospital, not here with no medication."

Her voice broke, and she turned away quickly, determined that he wouldn't see her tears. She was at the door, her hand on the knob, when Julian reached her side. His uninjured arm drew her to him as he said softly, "Easy, honey, I know you're worried about me, but I really am all right."

"Sure, wrestling crocs is just good, clean fun."

"Well, no, I wouldn't put it that way. Actually, they stink something awful. But I got off very lightly." Gently lifting her chin, he said, "Come on now, admit it. With your Mom's stitching and the fact that no germ would have the nerve to be caught in her house, I'll be fine in no time."

"And meanwhile you can't sleep."

"It does twinge a bit," he admitted reluctantly, "but that's only to be expected."

"You need to rest," she insisted. "How about if I go downstairs and get you a brandy."

"That applejack stuff your Dad makes?"

When she nodded, he laughed and said, "Okay, but don't fill the glass. As I recall, his home brew packs quite a wallop."

She hurried off, glad to be able to do him this small service. Downstairs in the kitchen she opened the cherry cupboard, found the stone crock where the brandy was kept and, disregarding Julian's instructions, filled a good-sized glass almost to the brim.

When she brought it back to him, he took one look and burst out laughing, only to quickly put a hand over his mouth to try to stifle the sound. "Are you looking to put me under for a few days?"

"Not at all," she said primly. "This is purely medicinal."

He laughed, took a sip, and coughed. When he spoke again his voice was hoarse. "Good batch." Mischievously he added, "Have a sip."

She backed away quickly, holding up her hands as she grinned. "No thanks. I don't have any excuse for doing that to my body."

"Mmmm, and such a nice body. It's a shame we're not at my place."

Her eyes widened. "You aren't seriously suggesting that you'd... With that arm?"

"No, actually with something else." When she turned bright red he had all he could do not to roar with laughter. "Honey, if we're going to be the least bit discreet, you'd better hightail your cute little butt out of here."

She sniffed and tossed her hair. "Has anyone ever mentioned that you talk like a chauvinist?"

He took another sip and eyed her narrowly, his gaze wandering over her slender figure, barely concealed by the thin nightgown. "Only you."

"H-rmph. How are you feeling now?"

He flexed his arm experimentally and took another sip. "Not bad. This stuff seems to do the trick."

"Good, how about getting into bed?" She smoothed the pillows on his bed and folded down the sheet invitingly. To do so she had to turn around, presenting him with an enticing view of the butt in question.

"If you're deliberately trying to torture me," he said huskily, "you're succeeding."

She didn't deign to comment. "I'll be going now."

"Yeah... you do that."

At the door she hesitated. "Julian... I just wanted to say... what you did was incredibly brave."

"Getting chewed on by a croc?"

"Saving my father. He could have been killed."

He shrugged dismissively. "Not Charlie. He's too tough. The croc would have taken one taste and spit him out."

Arlette stared at him for a moment, trying to find some way to express what she was feeling. She didn't have much luck. It was unlikely that he would ever admit the magnitude of what he had done.

She hesitated a moment longer, looking at him in the silvery light, then returned to her own bed where there was some small measure of safety, if not comfort.

Nine

The wedding celebration for Jeannie Devereux and Paul Rondale took place at the home of the bride's parents. The whole town turned out to wish the young couple good luck even though everyone agreed they were already very fortunate. Not only had Paul found a good job in the oil fields, but Jeannie was going to be teaching at the local school, at least until their first child came.

Besides some two dozen chickens, Jeannie received a full complement of towels, linens, pots, pans, dishes and assorted other household wares. Her father, her brothers, and various men from the town had joined together to build a small, cozy house on the edge of her family's property, near where it joined Paul's. There she and her husband would settle down to begin their life together.

But first there was the wedding feast.

Jeannie stood, smiling and blushing, beneath an oak tree on her parents' front lawn, where she received the guests as they arrived, thanked them for their gifts and invited them to enjoy themselves. Beside her, Paul looked tall, handsome and only slightly self-conscious.

Tables had been set out under the trees, near where the band would play all night. The wooden slabs supported by saw horses groaned under pots of gumbo, platters of seafood, baskets of bread, and all manner of Cajun specialties. Within easy reach, wash tubs loaded with ice and beer were covered in burlap to keep the precious cold in.

None of the guests needed to be told twice to dig in. Platters were quickly filled as hearty appetites demanded satisfaction. When Arlette bit into a slice of *boudin blanc*, a bloodless sausage made with rice and heavily seasoned, her eyes slitted with pleasure.

"I'd forgotten how good this is," she said to Julian, who sat beside her, doing full justice to his own meal. They had found two chairs a little bit away from the others and were enjoying their relative privacy.

"I've been to some of the fanciest restaurants in the world and I'd trade them all for this," he said. "Nothing beats good friends, good music and good food."

"I know exactly what you mean. The further I got away from this place, the more I needed to come back."

"That's because it's home."

He spoke so softly that it took her a moment to respond. A soft sigh escaped her. Her gaze wandered across the brown-green of the bayou lapping quietly, eternally at the shore, over the softly rolling lawn

dotted with ancient trees wreathed in vines, and farther to the heat-hazed blue sky that was the canopy
beneath which all her childhood dreams had un-
folded.

"Yes," she murmured, "it's home, even if I do only
half belong here."

"Are you sorry about that?"

"No... not exactly." She met his eyes, seeing in his
gaze more sympathy and understanding than she
would have hoped to find. "In a way I envy Jeannie.
She knows what she wants and where she belongs. It's
not so simple for me... or for you."

"We've both got one foot in the bayou and the
other in the world beyond," he agreed. "That position can get uncomfortable."

"Do you have any advice about what to do about
it?"

He grinned ruefully and shook his head. "'Fraid
not. There are some problems that simply defy solu-
tion."

"That doesn't sound very optimistic."

"Sure it is. If you work it right you can have the best
of both worlds."

"Maybe *you* can," she said quietly. "I'm not so
sure about myself."

He looked at her steadily for a moment before he
asked, "What's the matter, honey? Something seems
to really be getting you down."

Embarrassed at having revealed so much of herself, she glanced away. "I guess I'm a little unhappy
about leaving here and moving to New Orleans."

"But you wanted that job so much."

"I still do, but it's taking me away from my family
and my home. That's hard."

"You've always known there would be a high price to pay for what you want to achieve," he pointed out gently.

"Which I accept. It's just that..." She broke off self-consciously. "What I'm feeling doesn't make sense. I should be thrilled to finally be able to do the kind of work I've always wanted."

"And I'm sure you will be once you get started. Besides, living in New Orleans won't be so bad. We can come back here very often to see your folks."

We. Arlette turned the word over in her mind, savoring it. A single syllable, yet providing exactly the reassurance she needed. Her face brightened as she said, "That's true, and we can do all sorts of other things together. For instance, how about helping me look for an apartment this weekend?"

"We could do that...but I don't really see the point. Why don't you move in with me?"

Arlette looked at him in surprise. She hadn't expected him to be willing to make such a commitment so soon. "Living together is a big step," she said hesitantly.

"People do it all the time. Surely you're not going to try to tell me that we don't know each other well enough."

No, she wasn't about to try that, nor did she consider claiming that she didn't like the idea of living with him. Actually, she thought it would be heaven. She was simply a bit taken aback by how casual he seemed about it.

"What we've shared so far isn't quite the same as being in the same place day after day and...night after night."

"It's the last part that particularly interests me," he said with an engaging leer.

She shook her head wryly. "I know it's hard, but let's try, just for a moment, to keep our minds on something besides sex."

"Spoilsport."

Ignoring him, she went on firmly. "First, there's the matter of rent. How much do I pay you?"

A slight flush darkened his hard-boned cheeks. "Don't be ridiculous."

"I'm not. It's only fair that I help with my share of the expenses. What about food, utilities, other things like that? Then there's the question of basic ground rules. Who does the cooking, tidying up, shopping...?"

"For heaven's sake, we're talking about living together, not setting up a business. We'll figure it out as we go along."

"We'll also fight."

He eyed her narrowly. "I've got news for you: we do that already."

"But now we have separate places to go to cool off. If we're living together, we won't."

"So we'll learn a little self-restraint. It won't kill us."

He had an answer for everything, Arlette thought. No matter what doubts or questions she raised, he wasn't going to change his mind. And if the truth be told, the more she thought about it, the more it made sense to move in with him. Besides the fact that she simply wasn't looking forward to living alone again, it would give them a good opportunity to find out if the future might hold more for them than an affair.

Not that she was about to say any of that to Julian. She sensed that he knew as well as she did what living together would mean, and was willing to simply bide his time in the hope that it would all work out.

They finished their meal a short time later and, anxious to work off some of the food, made their way to the dance floor. Wooden boards had been set down over a large rectangle of grass, providing an ample surface for the foot-stomping folk dances everyone favored.

Not that they didn't enjoy other kinds as well. When the band swung into a slow, romantic number Arlette nestled contentedly in Julian's arms. Her mother had checked his wound that morning and pronounced it to be mending, but she was still careful not to bump against his shoulder or chest. He laughed at her concern, claiming he had already forgotten about the croc.

They moved so well together that she lost all track of their surroundings, aware only of the warmth of his big, lean body against hers, the security of his strength and nearness, and the soft flutters of her desire for him, never totally quiescent.

The music had ended several moments before either of them realized it. When they did they stepped apart, aware of the tolerant, amused glances of the other guests. Arlette flushed slightly, though Julian took it in stride. With her hand in his, they left the dance floor.

As they sat on the edge of the bayou, idly flicking small pebbles into the water and watching the ripples they caused, the silence drew out between them. Arlette became a bit uncomfortable with it and sought a distraction. "Have you decided which house to buy?" she asked at length.

"I'm leaning toward that first one we saw. Is it still your favorite?"

"Yes, but you shouldn't let that influence you."

"I will if I want to."

She shot him a surprised glance, followed quickly by a smile. "So mature."

"You haven't answered my question. Is that still the one you prefer?"

"Yes," she admitted. "I know some of the others were larger, and a few are in better shape, but there's just something about it...."

"Walking through there," he said slowly, "I got the feeling that the people who had once lived in those rooms had been happy."

She looked down at the strong hands stroking a water-smoothed pebble and nodded. "I felt that, too. It's a place that's known love."

He cupped the stone between his thumb and forefinger and skimmed it out over the bayou. It flew perhaps twenty yards, struck the water and bounced off three times before at last settling beneath the surface.

"I'll call the real estate agent," he said, "and make an offer."

"If you do get it," she warned, "there'll be a tremendous amount of work to do before you can move in."

He laughed and stood up, reaching for her hand again. "You didn't think those weekends I mentioned were going to be all fun, did you?"

They left for New Orleans at the end of that week. Arlette's parents said nothing about her plans to stay with Julian "while she got settled." She didn't imagine for a moment that they believed she would be sleeping in the guest room, but she appreciated their respect for her privacy and her judgment.

Of course, the fact that they thought so highly of Julian made it easier for them to accept her relationship with him. Yet she still wondered sometimes at their tolerance. Perhaps Louis had been right and attitudes were really changing in the bayou.

"You take care of yourself, honey," her mother said as they embraced on the porch steps.

"Call and let us know how you're getting on," her father requested.

She agreed, reassured them several more times that she hadn't forgotten anything, then got into the car. Her rental car had already been dropped off, so she no longer had to concern herself with it.

The day was clear and slightly cooler than usual. They were able to keep the windows rolled down instead of relying on the air conditioner. When they reached his apartment, Julian carried Arlette's bags upstairs and did not put them down until he had reached his bedroom.

At her hesitant glance toward the guest room, he said, "Don't even think about it. Now, do you want to unpack or get some dinner first?"

"Oh, I get to decide something, do I?" she asked with feigned innocence.

"Left to yourself you'd still be debating whether or not to move in here. Admit it; you need me to decide some things for you."

"Perhaps," she allowed with a faint smile. He looked so little-boy endearing, as though determined to cajole her into admitting that he had been right after all. "Just remember, something isn't the same as everything. There are going to be times when we disagree."

"Fine, then we can have fun making up."

Having settled the situation to his own satisfaction, if not completely to hers, he took her out to a fabulous dinner on the top floor of a hotel in downtown New Orleans from which they could see the entire panoply of the city spread out before them.

Afterward he took her back to the apartment, to his bed, and made long, slow love to her until she forgot everything except her love for him. The shattering pleasure he bestowed so generously on her made her long to please him in turn. Gently, patiently, he helped her to overcome her lingering hesitancy and taught her to know the secrets of his body as thoroughly as he knew hers.

In her first days of living with Julian, Arlette began to think he had been right. They got along so well together, sharing so much laughter and happiness, that she wondered how she could ever have hesitated to accept his offer.

It wasn't simply that they did so well in bed together; there was far more involved. Living together, Arlette quickly discovered, brought a level of intimacy she had never before experienced. In a multitude of small, ordinary ways she saw for herself how fair and reasonable Julian could be.

His housekeeper, a motherly black woman with a tolerant smile, came three times a week to clean, shop and prepare some meals. But even so, there were always little things that needed doing, from cleaning the table after a meal to hanging up damp towels in the bathroom and putting away clothes.

Not even once did Julian give any hint that he expected her to wait on him or tidy up after him. On the contrary, he was so relentlessly self-sufficient that Arlette was hard pressed to do even the slightest service for him. Only with the utmost reluctance did he allow her to replace a button that had popped off one of his shirts, after admitting sheepishly that his large fingers had never learned to hold a needle.

As the day approached for her to begin her new job she dared to think that all her problems might truly be behind her.

The headquarters of Oilcon, one of the six biggest energy companies, took up most of a fifty story skyscraper not far from the New Orleans Superdome. The offices of the research and development division were on one of the topmost floors, with breathtaking views of the city and the river beyond.

When she arrived that first morning, Arlette was met by Jim Davidson, head of the division and one of the men who had interviewed her. In his mid-fifties, with thinning red hair and sandy complexion, he was a genial man possessed of a steel backbone and wits sharpened by years in the field.

"We're glad to have you on board," he said as he showed her into the office near his own that she would use when working at headquarters. It was spacious and comfortably furnished, but she hoped she wouldn't be spending too much time there.

As though to confirm that, Jim said, "Don't get too comfortable. There's a meeting in half an hour to discuss new assignments, and I think you'll be pleased by the results."

Arlette nodded, not trying to contain her excitement. She spent the intervening time getting acquainted with several of the other staff members, all of whom seemed pleased to see her, though a bit startled by her sex.

She got that impression again when Jim introduced her at the start of the staff meeting. No one said anything directly, but the glances cast her way were a mixture of surprise and caution. She took them in stride, but was glad when the subject turned to the new assignments and everyone was quickly distracted.

Jim pulled a large roll-chart down on one wall and gestured to it as he explained the situation. "As most of you know, we've been doing some fairly extensive exploratory drilling on the underwater shelf fifty or so miles out in the Gulf. The results have been pretty good so far, and we've decided to step up our efforts. Several rigs that haven't been in use lately are going to be reactivated. That means they'll need crews."

There was a ripple of excitement around the table. Arlette felt it within herself, but was surprised it wasn't stronger. What Jim was saying meant that she would be given an immediate chance to help make a major oil find. That was exactly what she had worked so hard for, so why wasn't she happier about it?

The answer wasn't difficult to come by: assignment to an offshore rig meant that she would be away for at least a week at a time. Although Julian must certainly have known that was a possibility when she took the job, she didn't think for a moment that he would be pleased.

Yet when she told him after dinner that night as they were sitting in the living room, he merely shrugged and asked, "When do you have to leave?"

"Day after tomorrow," she said, her attention focused on his apparent lack of concern. That hurt her, though she tried her best to hide it.

At least he frowned a little at that. "They're not giving you much time to settle in."

"No, but then, this isn't the kind of assignment that can wait." Not quite sure who she was attempting to convince, him or herself, she said, "Besides, it won't be so bad. A lot of the guys are on two-week tours, whereas I'll be able to get back here nearly every week."

"How nice," he murmured dryly. "We'll be part-time roommates."

Arlette took a deep breath, summoning patience. He really was taking it very well; the least she could do was appreciate that. "I know the situation is hardly ideal, but I don't see any alternative, at least not at the moment."

"There is one," he said slowly, his eyes holding hers. "You could go to work for Petrex instead."

She wasn't really surprised by the suggestion; in fact, she had been half expecting it for some time. To gain a little breathing space she asked, "Has your takeover been completed, then?"

He nodded and reached for the snifter of brandy on the low table in front of them. "We signed the last papers this morning. The company is basically in good shape, despite its recent mismanagement. The only real area of neglect has been exploration. I'll be fielding several teams soon on our lease holdings in the Gulf, not very far from Oilcon's. There's no reason why you couldn't join one of them."

"But . . . what would that gain us? We'd still be separated a great deal of the time."

"Not necessarily. While I'll certainly be involved in the day-to-day management of Petrex, I'll be spending most of my time with the field teams. We could work together."

It was a very tempting idea—even Arlette had to admit that—but it also filled her with profound reservations. For one thing, she had already accepted the job with Oilcon.

"I can't just walk away from a position I've already committed myself to," she said quietly. "That wouldn't be ethical."

"No," he agreed reluctantly, "it wouldn't. But I'm sure that isn't your only concern."

He was certainly right there. The thought of working directly with Julian both excited and dismayed her. It would be so easy to slip back into the habit of deferring to his judgments and wishes, in essence, of letting him control her.

"I need a measure of independence from you," she said carefully. "Not in our personal lives; I don't mean that at all. But professionally, I have to prove myself without depending on you to do it for me."

"Because you still don't believe that I approve of your career." He spoke flatly, but with an underlying note of regret.

"I admit you haven't shown any objection since we got back together...."

"Yet you still don't trust me?"

"It isn't a question of trust," she insisted.

He turned and looked at her directly. His hazel eyes were heavily lidded, his expression unreadable. "Isn't it? I could have mentioned the job with Petrex before you joined Oilcon, but I didn't, because I was sure you would refuse. I kept hoping that if I waited a little while longer you'd come around to feeling differently about me, and yourself.''

"Julian," she said very softly, her hand instinctively reaching out to touch his prominent cheekbone in a gesture that was at once seductive and comforting, "you don't want me to feel different, not really. Why should you, when I already love you?"

He swallowed hard, the powerful muscles of his throat rippling with the force of his emotions.

She moved closer, unable to bear the thought that she was hurting him. Compared to that, even his seeming lack of concern was preferable.

"I love you," she said again, "but I don't want to be controlled by you. I want to share my life with you, not live it through you. Is that so hard to understand?"

"No," he admitted reluctantly, catching her hand in his and raising it to his lips. The touch of his mouth on her palm made her tremble. "But by the same token you can't expect me to be content with only a small part of you."

She looked away, wishing he wasn't touching her quite so gently, so persuasively. In a hushed voice she said, "I'm doing the best I can, Julian. Please try to be patient."

He sighed deeply. "I am trying, sweetheart, but believe me, it isn't easy. After all those years apart, I tend to want everything at once."

"So do I, but I'm afraid if we try to rush it we'll lose what we already have."

Julian took a deep breath. She had asked for his patience, and he would do his best to grant it, but the giving was not easy. On the contrary, he felt strained to the limit when he thought of all she was withholding. Wryly he acknowledged that she was not completely wrong to fear his intentions. As he had already admitted once, there was a part of him that really did want to own her. Frankly, he doubted that he would be completely a man if he wasn't capable of feeling like that.

Yet beyond the sheer male drive to possess were other, subtler needs. He wanted her not only as a woman, but also as the complex, fascinating, delightful person she was. Unless she was his friend as well as his lover he would never be satisfied.

Of course, he thought wryly, even if he did someday manage to win her completely, satisfaction would still elude him. No matter how many times or how thoroughly he had her, he would only want her all the more.

Even now, when he was genuinely angry about her stubborn insistence on following a course he believed was wrong, he longed to lose himself within her and to feel again the sweet surrender of her body.

"Arlette..."

"Hmmm..." she murmured, nestled against him. He had been quiet long enough for her to begin to feel a bit apprehensive, but the low caress of his voice reassured her.

"If you're leaving in two days, it seems foolish to waste what time we have."

She glanced up through the thick veil of her lashes. In the shadows cast by the single lamp beside the couch, the chiseled planes and angles of his face looked even sharper and more ruthless than usual. The simple white shirt he wore might have looked ordinary on another man, but on him it was anything but. He had removed his tie and jacket when he returned from the office, and undone the top buttons to reveal the springy dark curls dusting his chest.

Her fingers curled under as she stared at him, fighting the urge to touch what her eyes caressed. Anticipation, she already had learned, was an integral part of pleasure.

Her tongue darted out to moisten lips gone suddenly dry with excitement. Julian's gaze followed the unconscious motion. Under his breath he murmured, "You are a temptress who doesn't realize her power."

She frowned slightly, wondering if he was teasing. "What do you mean?"

He shook his head, a slight smile curving his hard mouth. "Oh, no, I'm not about to explain that. You have enough weapons against me as it is."

"I don't see how," she said faintly. "Next to you, I'm a novice."

"Sometimes," he murmured as he bent his head to her, "experience doesn't count anywhere near as much as instinct."

She returned his smile then, gaining in confidence. "Oh, well, if we're going to talk about instincts, I'll trust mine any day."

He stood up suddenly, taking her by surprise as he bent and lifted her high against his broad chest. She stiffened slightly, only to relax as the warm strength of his big, hard body enveloped her. "Actually, my sweet, we're not going to talk at all."

She had no objection to that, content to acquiesce as he laid her on the bed and made short work of both her clothes and his. When she did try briefly to help him, he stopped her, muttering under his breath, "Lie still."

Obeying, she was rewarded by the sight of his superbly fit body shorn of the trappings of civilization, gleaming bronze in the moonlight flowing through the bedroom windows. He was so large and muscular, at the peak of his virility, that he seemed almost a part of another time, when men struggled against the earth and each other. Then women were wise to tread carefully and become adept at the skills that turned anger to passion and violence to tenderness.

Far in the back of her mind it occurred to her that if she had been a woman in such an age, she would have naturally accepted Julian as her lord and master without hesitation. In fact, she would have counted herself lucky to do so, because in his strength would have been her own survival, and that of her children.

But now the world was different. Or at least so she wanted to believe.

As she lay naked on the bed before him a shiver of anxiousness ran through her. She felt almost unbearably vulnerable, yet she could not bring herself to make the slightest effort to protect herself. Not when those instincts she had boasted of told her she had absolutely nothing to fear from him.

Unless she counted the torrent of passion he unleashed within her when, with a groan, he lowered himself onto her waiting body and, without gentleness, but with incandescent passion, made her his.

Afterward, lying in his arms after he had fallen asleep, she listened to the rhythmic sound of his breathing and wondered at the wisdom of trying to resist such a man. As an adversary he was nothing short of terrifying. She did not want to fight him, yet neither did she want to surrender to him.

At least not unless she could be assured that his surrender matched her own.

Ten

Oilcon 5, the rig to which Arlette was assigned, was situated on the continental shelf some fifty miles southeast of New Orleans, not far from where the Mississippi flowed into the Gulf. Rising several hundred feet above the water, it was home to a crew of scientists and laborers who worked twelve-hour shifts as much to battle loneliness and boredom as to increase productivity.

It was not the first rig Arlette had been on, but arriving there by helicopter brought home to her once again the magnitude of man's effort to wrest energy from beneath the sea.

After being built some ten years before at a construction yard in Morgan City, the rig had been floated to its present location before being attached to underwater pylons driven far down into the sandy floor of the Gulf. In size and basic configuration it bore some resemblance to a gigantic aircraft carrier. On the starboard side, beneath the control tower, was a landing pad half the size of a stadium field. It served the copters that transported personnel back and forth in good weather. In bad weather, launches had to be used.

Because the rig was by no means new it was somewhat the worse for wear. Arlette told herself that she didn't mind; physical comforts were inconsequential when compared to the job she had come to do. But their lack only further aggravated the pain of missing Julian.

The best salve to that was work, and she threw herself into it without delay. Oilcon 5 was in the process of taking rock borings, seeking geological indications that might point to the presence of significant gas or oil. It was Arlette's job to analyze the hard-packed sediment brought up by the drills and make recommendations as to whether or not the site was worth further effort.

The task was complex and difficult, with so much riding on it that she naturally felt nervous about making a mistake. For her first few days she did little except stay in the lab, peering through microscopes, weighing samples, and doing her utmost to accurately evaluate the material she was given.

That there was oil below was not in doubt; the Gulf of Mexico, like the North Sea, parts of the Middle East and a few other places on earth, essentially floated on a sea of oil. But the sea was not uniformly deep. In some places the oil was so thinly spread as to make commercial retrieval impractical. In others it was so plentiful as to assure great riches for whoever found it first. The sites might be a fraction of a mile apart in distance, and hundreds of millions of dollars apart in profits.

To be able to tell where to drill and where not to bother from a handful of rock borings required superb training and iron nerve. Arlette had both, but even so she was more than a little nervous as she struggled over her first report.

At least the other members of her crew were proving to be helpful. All men, except for a middle-aged nurse on the medical team, they nonetheless welcomed her politely and soon made her feel, if not at home, at least not exactly a stranger.

Only one or two attempted to flirt with her, and they were quickly disabused of any ideas they might have had by her courteous but cool manner.

With so much to concern her, the first week sped by, yet she was still more than ready to board the helicopter returning her to shore. She longed to see Julian, to be with him again. The moment she set foot in their apartment she felt as though she had been gone a year instead of a week.

Julian wasn't yet back from the office, so she had time to bathe and start dinner before he returned. After soaking in the oversized whirlpool bath, she smoothed on a lightly scented moisturizing lotion, selected a sapphire silk robe that highlighted her eyes, then brushed her chestnut hair until it glistened.

With a smile of anticipation she hurried out to the kitchen to put the seafood bisque the housekeeper had made on the stove to simmer and begin fixing a salad. Before she was halfway through she heard the key turn in the lock and went to greet Julian.

He stood in the doorway for a moment, almost as though surprised to see her, and she had a chance to see how tired he looked. Then his shoulders straightened and he smiled as he reached for her.

"I was hoping you'd be here," he said huskily against the soft pillow of her hair.

"You knew I would be," she reminded him gently, her arms around his taut waist.

He drew back slightly and looked down at her, his expression unfathomable. "Sure, so what's for dinner?"

She rolled her eyes and laughed. "Just like a man. If you're so hungry, then come and help me get it on the table."

He followed her into the kitchen, but merely leaned against the counter, watching her as she took glasses and dishes from the cabinet. Passing him on her way to set the table, she raised an eyebrow. "Feeling like a gentleman of leisure?"

"No," he said softly, taking hold of her elbow and turning her to him. Gently but implacably he removed her burdens and set them down on the table. "As a matter of fact, I'm not feeling like a gentleman at all. And I'm not hungry, at least not for food."

"Oh..." Arlette licked her lips nervously. She wanted desperately to be with him, but the predatory gleam in his hazel eyes was almost frightening. Instinctively she took a step back only to be stopped by his hold on her.

"A week is a long time," he said flatly. "I need you."

Without further preamble he lifted her and strode into the bedroom. Arlette thought she really ought to say something, point out that she wasn't simply a toy to be used for his amusement, but the words stuck in her throat. They simply could not stand up against the sheer force of her need for him.

Blushing beneath his unrelenting gaze, she nonetheless stood straight and proud, returning his stare unflinchingly, until he said, "Take off your clothes."

"Wh-what . . . ?"

"Take them off. That robe looks delicate. I don't want to rip it." As he spoke he undid the knot of his tie and shucked off his jacket, then sat down on the chair near the bed and swiftly removed his shoes. All the while his eyes never left her.

"Julian . . . I don't think . . ."

"Good, I'd just as soon you didn't. Get undressed."

What on earth had come over him? If he was trying to make her extremely uncomfortable, he was succeeding brilliantly. "Now look . . ." she began, despising the tentativeness in her voice, but unable to suppress it.

He had stood up and removed his shirt. His hands were on the buckle of his belt as he paused, looking at her. "Of course, if you don't want to have sex, we can just forget it."

"H-have s—?" Her mouth dropped open; she could do nothing more than stare at him blankly. Never had Julian spoken to her so crudely; never had he made her feel like anything less than the woman he cared for deeply. Until now.

"You're angry," she said quietly when she had regained some control of herself. "My being away for a week has upset you, and this is how you're taking it out on me."

"Could we skip the junior psychologist bit?" he asked scathingly. "Either you want to or you don't. Which is it?"

Her eyes flashed dangerously as she gathered herself to her full height, a rather wasted effort, considering that he topped her by a head. "Since you're being so romantic and persuasive, how could I resist?"

When he looked momentarily surprised, she answered her own question as she stomped to the door. "Easily. If you want anything to eat, it will be on the stove."

She was halfway out of the room before he caught her and dragged her back, not gently. "Whatever else we do tonight, Arlette, we won't argue. I'm sorry if I offended your delicate sensibilities, but as you gathered, being without you for a week has not sweetened my temper."

"That's no excuse for—"

"No," he agreed, more gently, "it isn't. But I do need you very badly, and I think you need me."

She could hardly deny that, not when the nearness of his body was making hers tremble. Instinctively she raised a hand to his bare chest as though to push him away, only to have her touch become a caress.

"I have missed you," she murmured, "more than I ever expected. But it isn't just the lovemaking. I miss everything we share."

He took a deep breath, catching her hand with his and drawing her nearer. "So do I, sweetheart, and that scares me."

She smiled faintly. "I have a hard time imagining you afraid of anything."

"I'll admit it doesn't happen very often, which is just as well, since I'm not enjoying the experience."

"Oh . . ." Her eyes lifted to his. "Maybe we should do something about that."

"I'd appreciate it," he sad gravely. Releasing her, he stood back, silently allowing her to make her decision.

Arlette barely hesitated. She walked back into the room and over to the bed, which she matter-of-factly turned down. He continued to watch her, his arms folded over his broad chest, as she demurely removed her robe and folded it over the back of the chair. Beneath it she was naked.

Julian's breath caught in his throat. Though he had cherished the memory of her through each long and lonely night, he was still not fully prepared for the breathtaking beauty before him. All the driving force of his boundless spirit seemed to flow into his loins as he contemplated her slender loveliness. From the rose-tipped peaks of her breasts to the narrow span of her waist and hips to the fluid grace of her long legs, she was woman personified.

His response was immediate and unmistakable. Arlette cast a quick glance at him as he stripped off his remaining clothes; then she prudently dove under the covers and did not look at him again until he had joined her there.

"Bashful, sweetheart?" he murmured as he gently stroked the petal-smooth curve of her cheek. "Surely there's no reason to be."

Arlette gazed up at him helplessly, at a loss to explain her feelings. He was right in saying that lovers such as them should not be shy with each other. Yet she was, nonetheless. It was as though his overwhelming masculinity made her almost unbearably aware of her own womanliness, with all the implications she was not yet quite ready to acknowledge.

Determined to distract herself as much as him, she gently stroked her hands down his back, letting her fingers dig in slightly as she explored the steely line of muscle and sinew.

He groaned deep in his throat and arched, almost like a great jungle cat deigning to be petted. "Mmmm, that feels good.... A little to the left..."

She obliged and was rewarded with a rumbling in his chest that remarkably resembled a purr. The laughter that broke from her brought his eyes to her face. "What's so amusing, woman?" he asked in a threatening growl.

She laughed again and put her arms around him, hugging him close. "You are; I am; the two of us are. We find things to argue about even when we'd rather be..."

His mouth, taunted provocatively. "Yesss...?"

"You know what."

"No," he claimed with a perfectly straight face. "Tell me."

Her eyes glittered as she accepted the challenge. Moving against him so provocatively that he gasped, she murmured softly, "When we'd rather be making love."

"I certainly would be," he assured her fervently, his big hands moving downward to lightly clasp her breasts in callused palms. The rough abrasion of his touch made her tremble even as it filled her with delicious languor. He moved over her, his thigh thrusting gently between hers until they parted for him.

"Don't deny me, my love," he murmured against her throat.

To do so would be to deny herself. The generosity of unbridled love made her open her arms to him even as she opened her body. Their union was tumultuous and infinitely satisfying, but was no sooner over than both were in need again.

When Julian loved her this second time he was slower and more restrained, drawing out her passion until she thought she could not possibly endure it a moment longer. Only then did he bring her to shattering release, following swiftly as he groaned out her name.

Not until much later did they untangle themselves and venture into the kitchen to have dinner. Even then they could barely leave off touching and caressing. The meal was no more than half-eaten when, by unspoken agreement, they put the remainder away in the refrigerator before returning hand in hand to bed.

Arlette truly believed that she reached the heights of ecstasy that night in Julian's arms, but she was to discover quickly that such joy had a stiff price. Returning to the rig for her second duty tour was so painful that she literally ached inside with loneliness and the stirrings of undeniable doubt.

That was the pattern of their life for more than a month, as they met thrillingly, only to part again and again. Arlette prayed she would learn to accept it, but each time that she left Julian was harder than the last. It was all she could do to concentrate on her work when images of him crowded her mind and her body hungered for his touch.

Worse than any of that, however, were the questions that were beginning to gnaw at her. She had been so sure that she was doing the right thing when she took the job with Oilcon, yet if that was true, why was she so miserable?

Even as she told herself that only a silly child expected to be happy all the time, she couldn't help but think that no one who made the right decisions could possibly end up so disheartened. Each time she was home she was tempted to mention the possibility that she might have made a mistake to Julian, but pride prevented her from doing so. She still wasn't sure that he wouldn't lord her error over her, pointing out that he had known all along that she didn't really want what she claimed.

Her doubts became even more severe when, during one of her stays in New Orleans, Julian had to be away visiting a Petrex rig. He had done his best to avoid that, but this time his presence was absolutely essential. She spent a miserable few days alone in the apartment and was actually glad to get back to work that time.

The experience made her wonder all the more what it was like for him being there alone so much. To her doubt and concern was added guilt, a singularly unpleasant mixture.

Still she did her best not to let her work be affected, and she must have succeeded, because Jim Davidson did not hesitate to let her know how pleased he and the other executives at Oilcon were.

On a visit to the rig Jim caught up with her as she was examining a fresh boring just taken from the drill. Amid the heat and noise of the rig floor he waved to her and grinned.

"Hèy, Arlette, honey, over here. I want to talk with you for a minute."

With her hard hat pulled down over her ears she could barely hear him. When she did make out the words she nodded and, as soon as possible, went to join him.

It was very hot out on the platform, where the tool pushers worked stripped to the waist, their taut bodies dripping with sweat and stained with grease. Arlette knew several of the men fairly well now and sympathized with their discomfort, even though she knew she was in little better shape herself. The weather had been miserable for days now, hot and sultry, with the airlessness that sometimes presaged a bad storm.

As she walked toward Jim she glanced up at the sky, noticing that it was beginning to take on a yellow light that was faintly ominous.

"How's the report coming?" he asked as they climbed the steel ladder toward the main deck, where the dining hall was located. It was blessedly air conditioned, and they both breathed a sigh of relief as the coolness hit them.

"Pretty well," she assured him. They stood in line for a few moments to get cold drinks, then headed for a quiet table by the picture window overlooking the water. Normally the view was quite pleasant, but Arlette couldn't help but note that the Gulf was choppier than usual for that time of year.

Recalling herself to the subject at hand, she went on. "It's almost finished; I just need to add the final data. Basically what it will say is that I think there's substantial oil down there, certainly enough to justify further exploration."

Jim beamed her a smile and patted his round face with a handkerchief. "Thank heaven for that. I'd hate to think I sent you out here for nothing."

"Don't worry," she told him with a smile. "Whatever the outcome, it's been a real learning experience."

He must have caught the faintly tart note behind her words, because he frowned slightly. "The men haven't been giving you any trouble, have they?"

She shook her head and took a sip of her Coke, crunching the slivers of ice between her teeth.

"No, of course not. It's just that..." She hesitated, not sure how much to say. Since joining Oilcon she had become fairly well acquainted with Jim, enough to know that he was a devoted family man who had accepted a desk job at headquarters out of a desire to have more time with his wife and children. Perhaps, given that, he would be able to understand her predicament.

"I'm having some trouble reconciling my personal and professional commitments," she said at last. "Which is a fancy way of saying that the man in my life isn't too thrilled about my being away so much."

Jim nodded and sat back in his chair, surveying her. "Can't say that I blame him. If I were Julian, I'd be raising hell about the situation."

Arlette carefully shut her mouth lest flies get into it and said, "I suppose I really shouldn't be surprised that you know."

"The oil business is like any other; people gossip. I heard more than a month ago that Julian seemed to have finally met his match." He grinned and flattened his empty cup. "Couldn't happen to a nicer guy."

"He is a nice guy," Arlette said softly. With a wry tilt of her head she added, "Underneath it all."

"He's not a man I'd cross," Jim told her flatly. "Anybody who comes up from nowhere to take over a major oil company, then speedily goes about the process of rebuilding it, is a force to be reckoned with."

"He does have a tendency to get what he wants," she said dryly.

"And that's what worries you?" At her startled glance, he laughed. "I've got two daughters, one about your age. It's no news to me that women still have a tougher time than men combining a career with a family. Some men don't mind playing second fiddle, though I must say I can't see Julian doing that."

"I'm not asking him to...or at least I didn't think I was. Now I'm not so sure." Stubbornly she added, "If I were a man, everyone would expect me to put my job first."

"Would they? I did that for years, and where did it get me? Oh, sure, I earned a higher salary than I might have otherwise, but I also missed seeing my kids grow up and became pretty much a stranger to my wife. If I had it all to do over, you can bet some things would be different."

That gave her food for thought throughout the rest of the day as she completed her report. By the time she had done so word was circulating through the rig that a major storm was expected. Along with everyone else, she helped secure equipment and generally batten down.

"It's unusual to have a big blow at this time of year," Jim said later when she joined him for dinner. Food on the rig might be served cafeteria-style, but since it provided one of the few distractions on long tours, it was worthy of the finest restaurant. Generally Arlette found that she had a hearty appetite. That particular evening, however, was an exception.

With waves lashing against the windows of the dining hall, she couldn't muster enthusiasm for more than a bowl of soup and a few crackers. Jim noted her caution and said, "Don't tell me you aren't a good sailor."

"No, it isn't that. I'm just not crazy about storms."

"I know what you mean. After you've been through a few they tend to lose their glamour."

"Are we in for a bad one?" she asked quietly when they had reached their table.

"I don't know," he admitted. "The meteorology reports out of New Orleans are fairly uncertain. There's a major storm system heading toward us, but it could veer off or stall before it gets here."

"On the other hand, it could hit."

He shrugged, and sliced into a steak liberally smothered with onions and mushrooms. "This rig is built to withstand gale force winds and up. It would take a hell of a storm to make us evacuate."

"That's good. I don't much relish the idea of trying to get away from here in severe weather."

"I did it once," he said. "About ten years ago. One of the worst hurricanes ever to hit this area was expected to miss us by a good hundred miles, but instead struck head on. The copters couldn't fly, of course, and for a while we debated trying to stick it out, but there was no chance of that."

"Why not?" she asked, though she wasn't sure she wanted to know.

"It's the pylons," he explained, buttering a roll. "They can only take so much pressure. When it gets too bad they start to crumble."

Arlette put her spoon down and carefully did not look out the window. She hadn't considered the possibility of a pylon cracking, though now that she thought about it, she knew she had heard of such things. They were among the greatest fears of drillers anywhere, because a cracked pylon meant a floundering rig, awash in raging seas with its crew clinging helplessly as they sank into the sea.

She forced that possibility out of her mind, determined not to think of it anymore. Yet the fear returned again and again throughout that evening and into the night in which no one even tried to sleep.

Eleven

The storm hit in its full fury shortly before dawn. It tore at the rig as though determined to avenge the effrontery of man in daring to trespass on nature's kingdom. The wind howled so loudly that conversation was impossible. Arlette found it difficult to even hear her own thoughts as she worked with the other members of the crew trying to stem the storm's damage.

Despite their preparation there was really no way to prevent the effects of such an assault. Heavy equipment burst its lashings and careened across the deck, smashing into anything in its path before slamming through the railings and falling into the sea.

After watching a forklift meet that fate Arlette was grateful that her offer to take her turn with the crews working outside had been firmly rejected. Much as she hated to admit it, she quailed at even the thought of venturing into such turmoil.

At least she was able to assist the medical team, which was busy administering first aid to the ever-increasing number of casualties. With only one doctor and one nurse, they were hard-pressed to keep up with the flow of injuries and were glad of her support.

During a brief lull in the wind she was bandaging the head of a young man who'd been struck by a flying bolt. "Hell of a storm, ma'am," he said dazedly, "if you'll pardon my language. I sure do wish they could have gotten us out of here before it hit."

"So do I," she said quietly. "But I'm sure it will be over soon."

He cast her a skeptical look. "Don't think so, ma'am. I heard they got a report from New Orleans that it may last at least another full day."

"Another day...?" She paled and had to take a deep breath to steady her hands. How could they possibly withstand such a relentless pounding for another twenty-four hours? There would be nothing left of the rig before this was over.

The young man must have been thinking along similar lines, for he said, "I hear Davidson's on the radio to the Coast Guard, trying to figure out some way to get us off."

A quick glance around confirmed that Jim was indeed not in the dining room hall, which had become the center of operations in fighting the storm. Arlette could not recall seeing him for the last half hour or so.

"Do you think they'll be able to do that?" she asked quietly as she finished securing the bandage and handed him a hot cup of tea liberally laced with sugar to help counteract shock.

He shrugged, trying hard to look as though he wasn't particularly concerned one way or the other. But his words gave the lie to that. "Take a look at those waves, ma'am. Who's going to be crazy enough to come after us when they could get drowned for their trouble?"

Who indeed? The resources of the Coast Guard would be stretched to breaking by the sudden storm that had undoubtedly endangered people all over the Gulf. They would certainly try their best, but there were limits to what they could achieve. Reaching and evacuating a rig with more than fifty crew members might be too much.

When Jim returned to the dining hall a few minutes later the look on his face warned Arlette that she was right. His normally ruddy complexion was washed out, and the mouth she was used to seeing curved in a smile was drawn in a tight line.

He walked over to her, nodded and helped himself to coffee from the urn. After taking several sips and glancing around to be sure they couldn't be over-heard, he said, "We've got a problem."

"I noticed," she murmured.

"Yeah, guess it's pretty hard to miss." He ran a hand through his thinning hair and sighed wearily. "Damn it, we should have been out of here hours ago, and we would have been if meteorology had come through."

"You can't blame them," Arlette said, taking his cup from him to refill it. She was worried about Jim. He was middle-aged, somewhat overweight, and under immense strain. Technically the captain was responsible for the safety of everyone on board the rig. But Jim was the senior executive present, and much of the burden was bound to fall on him. "This storm is following a very unusual path, isn't it?" she asked. "Maybe it will veer off."

"And maybe cows will fly. No, I'm afraid we're really in for it."

She bit her lip, hoping he wouldn't see how his words affected her. If Jim was truly frightened, the situation had to be even worse than she had guessed. "Surely the rig was constructed to survive a storm like this," she ventured.

"Of course it was—ten years ago. Since then it's been through a hell of a lot." He broke off and stared into his coffee for a moment before abruptly pulling himself together and giving her a faint smile. "Forget what I said, honey. I'm just tired. We'll come through fine."

Arlette wasn't so sure, but since there was nothing she could do about it, she distracted herself as best she could by continuing to help the medical team and doing whatever else was needed. Several hours passed. The storm continued to grow in ferocity even as the injuries of the men stumbling into the dining hall became more serious.

Toward noon Jim and the captain appeared in the dining hall. Jim carried a bullhorn, the only way he could be heard over the howling of the wind. When he had everyone's attention he said, "There's no point beating around the bush, so I'm going to give it to you straight. We've got indications that at least one of the pylons is cracking. You all know what that means."

As the men looked from one to another grimly, he went on, "Meteorology tells us that the eye of the storm is due to pass over in about an hour. At that time a rescue force is going to make a run for us and try to get us off."

Quick murmurs passed through the crowd, surprise mingling with apprehension. Who were the men risking their lives to come after them?

"The Coast Guard is involved, of course," Jim explained. "But basically it's oil men, guys who happened to be on shore when the storm hit." He smiled faintly. "I guess they can't stand to miss the fun."

There was scattered laughter at that, undercut by tension. In the mind of each man had to be the thought that, but for the luck of the draw, he might have been one of those safe on shore, giving up that safety to try to rescue the less fortunate.

With the announcement that the rig was to be abandoned, frantic activity ensued. Everyone hurried to pack what few belongings could be taken as the wounded were strapped to stretchers and vital equipment was prepared for transport.

There was nothing in her cabin that Arlette especially wanted, except for a photo of Julian taken during one of their house-hunting expeditions. She couldn't bear the thought of leaving it to the mercy of the storm.

Making her way down the corridor to her quarters, she was forced to brace herself against the walls. What had once been a straight hallway now sloped dangerously. At one point she actually had to grab hold of a doorknob to keep herself from being flung to the floor.

Continuing on gingerly, she at last reached her goal and pushed open the door, having to bring all her weight to bear against it. When it finally gave, she was careful to prop it open with the metal chair that went with the small, pull-down desk.

The photo was on top of the desk. She glanced at it quickly, trying hard not to think of the possibility that she might never see Julian again. Her hands shook as she put the photo in the inside pocket of her windbreaker, pulled the zipper shut and climbed over the chair and back out of the cabin.

As she did so the rig gave a sudden lurch that sent her tumbling down the corridor. For a seemingly endless moment she feared she was going to lose consciousness. Colored lights splintered before her eyes as whirling darkness threatened to engulf her. Only with the greatest effort was she able to stagger to her feet and make her way down the rest of the corridor.

When she returned at last to the dining hall she found preparations almost complete for the evacuation. The wind was beginning to die down, signaling the arrival of the eye, that island of calm at the center of the storm. Anxious gazes scanned the sea, looking for any sign that the rescue boats were arriving.

When the first of them at last appeared, a ragged cheer went up. Eagerly, but in an orderly fashion, the men lined up and began making their way out on deck. It was still raining, though with nothing like the ferocity of a short time before. As the cold drops hit her face Arlette shivered. The dull throbbing in her temple was growing worse. She raised a hand to her forehead absently, then moaned faintly when it came away red with blood.

There was no time to try to find a bandage, or in fact to do anything at all. Hardly aware any longer of what was happening, Arlette felt herself pressed forward by strong hands and thrust into the seemingly fragile basket that was the only means of reaching the boats. Hoisted up and down at the end of a crane, it was uncomfortable, dangerous and occasionally a quick route to a cold dip.

Arlette instinctively curled her fingers around the mesh sides, holding on for dear life as she was yanked up into the air from the deck of the rig, slung out over the side and dropped without ceremony onto the nearest boat. The landing was bone jarring, and she moaned again as she tried to right herself.

Before she could do so she was seized in arms that were not at all gentle and dragged to her feet. Opening her mouth to protest, she gazed up numbly into Julian's taut features, devoid now of all gentleness or comfort.

"Get below," he ordered tersely.

The wind was increasing again. It tore at his ebony hair and plastered the black rain slicker he wore against his whipcord-taut frame. A dark flush suffused his hard-boned cheeks, and his eyes glittered with an unholy light.

Dazedly Arlette did as he said. She found her way below, where there were several small cabins clustered around a compact gallery. Her senses were whirling mercilessly as she fumbled her way into the nearest one and collapsed on the bunk. The pounding in her head grew worse. A low sob escaped her as she turned her injured head into the pillow and gladly slipped into unconsciousness.

When she came to it was oddly quiet. Not the ominous silence of the storm's brief pause that only warned of further havoc to come, but a genuine tranquility made all the more profound by what had gone before. It was still raining, but the sound of drops hitting the windows was oddly pleasant.

Windows? Gingerly Arlette opened first one eye, then the other. It was night; by the glow of a soft lamp she could make out details of the room in which she lay. It was far too large to be the cabin on the boat; moreover, it wasn't moving. She was on land.

Lifting her head, she winced at the pain but persevered until she had managed to raise herself on her elbows and glance around. As she recognized the familiar details of Julian's bedroom her hands clenched. Nervously, she swung her legs over the side of the bed and, summoning all her strength, managed to stand. As she did so she realized that she was naked and reached for the sheet, trying to pull it off to wrap around herself. But even that small effort was beyond her.

She had just given up and was trying to figure out what to do next when the door suddenly opened and Julian strode into the room. At the sight of her he froze, but only briefly. Recovering swiftly, he crossed to her side and took hold of her arms.

"What do you think you're doing?" he demanded.

She twisted in his hold, trying to break free, though she knew the effort was futile. Even normally her strength was no match for his; in her present weakened state she had no chance against him. "I'm looking for my clothes," she gasped. "What have you done with them?"

"They're drying in the bathroom," he said, his eyes raking over her slender form. What he saw made his scowl deepen even further. Sweeping her up in his arms despite her low moan of protest, he laid her on the bed and pulled the covers back over her firmly. "If you think I'm letting you go anywhere, you're out of your mind. You're not moving from this bed until I say so, and then it's only going to be so that I can tan that lovely little butt of yours."

Arlette gazed up at him bemusedly. He had risen from beside the bed and was pacing back and forth, his hands clasped tightly behind his back, as though he couldn't trust himself not to immediately carry out his threat.

"I've had it, Arlette," he grated hoarsely. "All these weeks of trying to be a nice, reasonable guy, go along with what you want, be understanding and liberated, and what did it get me?" Turning, he glared down at her so fiercely that her breath caught in her throat. "I almost lost you," he went on tautly, hardly able to say the words, yet driven to do so by forces beyond his control. "You could have been killed out there. Do you have any idea how that makes me feel?"

She wet her lips nervously, wishing she could look away from him, but unable to do so. Hesitantly, she whispered, "I'm sorry."

"You should be. The strongest, most experienced men are lucky to escape a storm like that alive. It's a miracle you got off with nothing but a bruised head."

She had forgotten about that. Lifting her hand to her forehead, she encountered the stiff folds of a bandage. "You might have had a concussion," he went on, not taking his eyes from her. "They were going to keep you overnight at the hospital, but I convinced them to let me look after you instead.''

His face paled beneath his burnished tan as he remembered that moment when he had found her lying in the cabin, unconscious and breathing shallowly. All efforts to revive her had failed, although now he realized that was simply because she had been so completely exhausted. At the time he had not been sure what to think, and the fear had been worse than anything he had ever known.

"I blamed myself for not noticing that you were hurt when I pulled you out of the basket," he said. "But I had been so afraid of not finding you that I couldn't think of anything else."

"It doesn't matter," she murmured, driven by some instinct she could not quite understand to comfort and reassure him. Her slender hand reached out to his. "Julian," she murmured weakly, "I know you were worried about me. I'm sorry. What more can I say?"

He took a deep breath and sat down on the edge of the bed, not touching her, but close enough so that she could feel the warmth of his body.

Sometime since bringing her home he had changed into dry clothes. The thin-knit shirt he wore hugged the massive sweep of his chest, while the well-worn jeans emphasized the narrow tautness of his waist and hips. There were shadows under his deep-set eyes, and lines etched into the planes of his face.

Arlette's heart twisted as she saw the mute evidence of his pain. "Please..." she said breathlessly, yearning to reach out to him once more, but afraid to do so lest he reject her again. "Listen to me.... I've done a lot of thinking the last few weeks. I know I was wrong to fear becoming dependent on you. Worse, I was lying to myself to even think it was possible to avoid doing so.''

He did not move or change his expression in any way, but she sensed he was listening to her intently. "What do you mean?"

"I didn't understand what it was to really love someone," she admitted, unaware that tears were gathering in her luminescent eyes and beginning to trickle down her pale cheeks. "It was frightening to me to need you so much. I kept fighting against that, trying to control and restrain it. I felt driven to prove to you that I was a strong, capable person in my own right."

"You never had to prove that," he said quietly. "I've always known it. Why do you think I love you so much?"

"I don't know," she admitted with a damp smile. "It certainly can't be because I'm so easy to get along with."

He laughed suddenly, a deep, male sound that sent a tremulous spurt of happiness through her. "That's the truth," he said, "but then, I'm no paragon myself." His gaze met hers as he touched a blunt-tipped finger to her cheek, gently wiping away a tear. Almost in a whisper, he asked, "Do you have any idea what we can do about this?"

"Well . . . we could try compromising."

He frowned, but did not withdraw his hand. "What would that involve?"

She swallowed against the dryness in her throat, wanting only to be in his arms, experiencing once again the incandescent pleasure she now realized was merely the most outward manifestation of their love. But before that could happen they had to reach some kind of understanding.

"I need to work," she said softly. "It's important to me. Oh, I won't necessarily always want to do it, especially if we were to have children. But right now I feel I have an important contribution to make in my field."

"Jim Davidson told me about your analysis of the test borings." At her questioning look he explained. "I ran into him at the hospital. He was having chest pains, and the people with him got the wind up, but it turned out he was okay. Anyway, we got to talking, and he told me what a terrific job you'd done." His gaze narrowed slightly as he added, "He also told me how bad he felt about endangering you."

"He hardly did it deliberately," Arlette protested.

"No, but he was putting himself in my place and imagining how he would feel if the woman he loved ended up in that kind of situation."

"I can understand that..." she said slowly, "and I know that if our positions had been reversed, if you'd been on the rig instead of me, I'd have been terrified. But the fact that I want to keep working doesn't mean I'd ever get caught in something like that again."

"No, but you could be transferred any place in the world and be away for months at a time."

"Not if I had a boss who happened to be very accommodating...."

He stiffened slightly, his hand suddenly tense against her delicate skin. His fingers slid down along her jaw to cup her chin, holding her in a firm but implacable grip as he looked at her steadily. "Did you have anyone in particular in mind?"

"Well, since I seem to be so good at what I do, it would have to be someone who was willing to meet my price."

"Salaries at Petrex are certainly competitive with the rest of the industry," he informed her, a hint of a smile beginning to curve his hard mouth.

"I was thinking more along the lines of fringe benefits," she informed him pertly.

"I'm instituting an excellent medical plan."

"Nice, but boring. What else can you offer?"

He leaned forward slightly, his lips brushing her throat. "How about long, languorous nights of lovemaking, days filled with companionship and laughter, and the chance to build a future together?"

Several moments passed before Arlette could answer. When she did so, her voice shook. "That sounds pretty good. How about if I were to offer the same thing? Do you think we could make a deal?"

"I'd certainly be willing to try," he said as he began to gently draw the sheet down from her breasts. Unexpectedly he stopped and smiled crookedly. "Just one other thing. I think you should know that your family is already planning the wedding."

"Since when?"

"Since I told them I wanted to marry you." A bit sheepishly he added, "Remember that first day when we ran into each other in town and I drove back with you and Louis? While you were upstairs changing we all had a chat and decided that this time around I wasn't going to lose you."

"Then they've known all along...?" she asked incredulously.

He nodded. "In fact, they've been a tremendous help. Not only did your parents tolerate our living together, since they knew I intended that to be very brief, but Louis even played Cupid by disabling your car so I could drive you into New Orleans."

"I wondered about that," she admitted. "It seemed a bit too convenient."

"Worked out pretty well, though."

"Hmmm...I suppose so." She sighed tolerantly and wrapped her slim arms around his neck, drawing him to her. "It's just lucky for you that I'm such a good-natured person."

"I can think of a few other reasons why I'm lucky," he said, drawing the sheet the rest of the way off so that he could feast on the sight of her nudity.

Though she flushed slightly, she made no effort to cover herself. Instead she reached for the buttons of his shirt and impatiently began to undo them. Halfway through, she said, "You know, none of this means that we won't still disagree sometimes. There are bound to be times when we argue."

"Sure," he agreed unconcernedly, "I wouldn't want it any other way. Being married to you promises to never be boring. Besides," he added as he obligingly shucked off his shirt, followed by his shoes and jeans, "isn't it fun to make up?"

She grinned mischievously. "Fun doesn't quite describe it. However, I think we could do with less talk and more practice."

"Action," he corrected with a smile. "The expression is less talk and more action."

She stretched languidly beneath him, her eyes slumberous with passion. "My point exactly."

His powerful chest rumbled against her as he eased himself tenderly into her embrace. Outside the rain continued to splatter against the windows as the storm slowly blew itself out. Inside it was very quiet except for the sighs and moans of lovers finding in each other the fulfillment of their most cherished dreams.

OFFICIAL SWEEPSTAKES INFORMATION

1. **NO PURCHASE NECESSARY.** To enter, complete the official entry/order form. Be sure to indicate whether or not you wish to take advantage of our subscription offer.

2. Entry blanks have been pre-selected for the prizes offered. Your response will be checked to see if you are a winner. In the event that these are not claimed, a random drawing will be held from all entries received to award not less than $150,000 in prizes. This is in addition to any free, surprise or mystery gifts which might be offered. Versions of this sweepstakes with different prizes will appear in Torstar Ltd. mailings and their affiliates. Winners selected will receive the prize offered in their sweepstakes insert.

3. This promotion is being conducted under the supervision of Marden-Kane, an independent judging organization. By entering the sweepstakes, each entrant accepts and agrees to be bound by these rules and the decisions of the judges which shall be final and binding. Odds of winning in the random drawing are dependent upon the total number of entries received. Taxes, if any, are the sole responsibility of the prize winners. Prizes are non-transferable. All entries must be received by August 31, 1986.

4. This sweepstakes package offers:

1, Grand Prize	: Cruise around the world on the QEII	$100,000 total value
4, First Prizes	: Set of matching pearl necklace and earrings	$ 20,000 total value
10, Second Prizes	: Romantic Weekend in Bermuda	$ 15,000 total value
25, Third Prizes	: Designer Luggage	$ 10,000 total value
200, Fourth Prizes	: $25 Gift Certificate	$ 5,000 total value
		$150,000

Winners may elect to receive the cash equivalent for the prizes offered.

5. This offer is open to residents of the U.S. and Canada, 18 years and older, except employees of Torstar Ltd., its affiliates, subsidiaries, Marden-Kane and all other agencies and persons connected with conducting this sweepstakes. All Federal, State and local laws apply. Void in the province of Quebec and wherever prohibited or restricted by law. Winners will be notified by mail and may be required to execute an affidavit of eligibility and release which must be returned within 14 days after notification. Canadian winners will be required to answer a skill testing question. Winners consent to the use of their names, photograph and/or likeness for advertising and publicity purposes in conjunction with this and similar promotions without additional compensation. One prize per family or household.

6. For a list of our most current prize winners, send a stamped, self-addressed envelope to: WINNERS LIST, c/o Marden-Kane, P.O. Box 10404, Long Island City, New York 11101.

AMERICAN TRIBUTE

Where a man's dreams count for more than his parentage...

Look for these upcoming titles under the Special Edition American Tribute banner.

CHEROKEE FIRE
Gena Dalton #307—May 1986
It was Sabrina Dante's silver spoon that Cherokee cowboy Jarod Redfeather couldn't trust. The two lovers came from opposite worlds, but Jarod's Indian heritage taught them to overcome their differences.

NOBODY'S FOOL
Renee Roszel #313—June 1986
Everyone bet that Martin Dante and Cara Torrence would get together. But Martin wasn't putting any money down, and Cara was out to prove that she was nobody's fool.

MISTY MORNINGS, MAGIC NIGHTS
Ada Steward #319—July 1986
The last thing Carole Stockton wanted was to fall in love with another politician, especially Donnelly Wakefield. But under a blanket of secrecy, far from the campaign spotlights, their love became a powerful force.

AM-TRIB-1R

AMERICAN TRIBUTE

American Tribute titles now available:

RIGHT BEHIND THE RAIN
Elaine Camp #301—April 1986
The difficulty of coping with her brother's
death brought reporter Raleigh Torrence
to the office of Evan Younger, a police
psychologist. He helped her to deal with
her feelings and emotions, including love.

THIS LONG WINTER PAST
Jeanne Stephens #295—March 1986
Detective Cody Wakefield checked out
Assistant District Attorney Liann McDowell,
but only in his leisure time. For it was the
danger of Cody's job that caused Liann to
shy away.

LOVE'S HAUNTING REFRAIN
Ada Steward #289—February 1986
For thirty years a deep dark secret kept them
apart—King Stockton made his millions while
his wife, Amelia, held everything together.
Now could they tell their secret, could they
admit their love?

 Silhouette Desire

COMING
NEXT MONTH

CHOICES—Annette Broadrick
Despite his blindness, Damon could sense the beauty of the woman
nursing him after his auto accident. But Elise had been hurt once by
divorce. Could he cure her fear of love?

NIGHT TALK—Eve Gladstone
Not just the airwaves crackled when WRBZ hired "Big Gun" Casey
Phillips to clean up its programming. Although Julie's talk show was
on his hit list, the electricity between them couldn't be denied!

KNOCK ANYTIME—Angel Milan
When a portion of Trina Taylor's novel wound up in Jonathan
Castle's computer files, the exchange of data seemed disastrous. But
in clearing up the mess they found their languages deliciously
compatible.

PLAYING THE GAME—Kathleen Korbel
Kelly enjoyed posing as heartthrob Matt Hennessey's "latest," and
his passionate attentions only helped. But when his real flame arrived
in town, Kelly knew she was playing with fire....

YESTERDAY AND TOMORROW—Candace Adams
Different backgrounds had separated them before, but when Jay
returned a successful businessman, that old excuse didn't hold water.
Could Cynthia forget her mother's prejudice and follow her heart?

CATCHING A COMET—Ann Hurley
Charlie Wilde was guiding a Baja Wilderness Trip in search of
adventure, but he soon ran headlong into Andromeda, a blue-eyed
natural phenomenon more exciting than his wildest dreams!

AVAILABLE NOW:

GREEN FIRE
Stephanie James

DESIGNING HEART
Laurel Evans

BEFORE THE WIND
Leslie Davis Guccione

WILLING SPIRIT
Erin Ross

THE BLOND CHAMELEON
Barbara Turner

CAJUN SUMMER
Maura Seger